# RISE OF THE PHENOTEENS

## KARI LEE TOWNSEND

OLIVERHEBERBOOKS

# 1

## "THE LETTER"

"Congratulations, Samantha Marie Granger," I slowly read out loud and blinked. "You are hereby invited to join us at the prestigious Institute of Phenomenon Research for gifted students in Washington, D.C."

I'd come downstairs for breakfast on the morning of what I'd thought would be just another boring average day. After the crazy rollercoaster ride adventure I'd just gotten off, normal and boring were a welcome relief. Except Dad was here today, and that could only mean one thing....

Something big was about to happen.

Glancing at my parents and Gram, I raised a brow, but they just stared at me all excited like. I swear if they were puppies, their tails would be wagging faster than my thumbs typing a text message. I frowned and kept reading the letter of doom he'd brought with him.

"Entrance into IPR is by invitation only. With the recent onset of your photographic memory, as well as the impressive way you handled the infamous Blue Lake showdown, we feel you are more than qualified." I clutched the letter in my hands, trying not to shake. This could not be happening to me. I refused to *let* it happen.

Taking a breath, I continued, "At IPR you will receive a top notch education as well as help in how to tap into the full potential of your gift. You are part of a select group of students we have chosen to test a new class we'd like to add to our program; therefore, your tuition has been waved. We urge you to respond soon as slots fill up quickly. Once again, congratulations. We look forward to hearing from you."

I looked up at Mom, Dad, and Gram in disbelief, and the first flicker of doubt crossed their faces. Good, because there was no way I was moving again. I planted my feet, put my hands on my hips, and simply said, "No," in four different languages.

Mom's excited smile vanished and her bright, sparkly blue eyes narrowed as she spoke in that stern, top-executive voice of hers. "What do you mean no? Last I checked you still live under my roof."

The air filled with tension until finally she smoothed back her perfectly styled, sleek blond bob. Forcibly relaxing her features, she closed her eyes for a minute before opening them once more. "Honey, I'm only doing what I think is best for you. I've researched this institute, and it really is an outstanding school."

"I won't go. You can't make me go." I looked at Dad--a laid back, big softy of a guy who was much easier to sway than Mom--and put on my best Daddy's-little-girl face. He just stared at me with that tolerant, patient look, and I knew I'd never win. I shook my head hard, my trademark medium brown ponytail swinging below my pink, flannel-jammy covered shoulders. I was toasty warm, but that didn't stop me from shivering. "She can't make me go, right?" I whined.

He blew out a breath, running a hand through his messy

brown hair. "I'm afraid I'm with her on this one, sweetie. Sorry. We cancelled the neurological tests because you seemed better, but we're still concerned. You've been through a lot, kiddo. I think this might be a great opportunity for you to come to terms with all that's happened."

"That's not fair. You both promised when we relocated to the Adirondacks, I wouldn't have to move again. I finally have friends, and you want to take that away from me? Gram, you have a photographic memory, and you never went away to some special school. Tell them I'll be fine."

"It took me a long time to get a handle on my gift, Sammy. I didn't have anyone to help me like you do." A pair of brown eyes the same shade as mine held me captive. "Your *gift* is much bigger than mine. Let someone who knows what they're doing help you figure it all out."

"Samantha, you're reading this all wrong." Mom took the letter from me and scanned the paper. She paced across the Persian throw rug in the formal living room of the massive contemporary house her company, Electro Corp, had rented for us.

"No one's asking you to move there permanently. You'd only be going away for a marking period. Just until you fully understand how your body has changed. It's not every day someone suddenly has a photographic memory, let alone a thirteen year old. This gift could open so many doors to your future if you'd just learn how to use it properly."

They had no idea just how much my body had "truly" changed since I'd touched that stupid glowing meteorite and my Electro Wave cell phone had fused with my central nervous system. A photographic memory wasn't even close to what my body could do now that I had a top secret military weapon inside me.

My best friend Mel and Gram were the only two who

knew I was Digital Diva. But after I outsmarted two terror-
ists during the showdown mentioned in the letter, my superhero days were over, thank goodness. I, for one, couldn't be
happier.

"Whatever happened to the land of the free? This is _my_
life." I tapped my chest. "Shouldn't that mean I have a say in
how I live it?"

All three stared at me until Dad finally spoke. "Why
don't we think it over today, and we'll talk about this
tomorrow."

Mom's jaw fell open and she started to speak, but Dad
held up his hand.

"We might be separated, Victoria, but I still have a say in
what goes on around here. I want to look into this _special_
class a little more before we send our daughter anywhere."
He gave her a pointed look, and for once, Mom backed
down. Dad finished with, "I know just who to go to for
help."

Mom pursed her lips, her cheeks flushing with obvious
irritation, but she nodded once in her sharp, brisk way. "Fine,
Wally. It's a good idea," she reluctantly admitted. "I trust
Agent Maxwell. He'll know just what to do since he's the one
who brought this school to our attention in the first place."

Dark Shades Man?

My breathing picked up a notch. I hadn't seen him since
the "showdown" last fall. I'd found a box with a new Digital
Diva costume inside, and then received a text that said the
government would be in touch. I'd suspected instantly that
it had come from Agent Maxwell. A sinking sensation grew
in the pit of my stomach. Was this his way of getting in
touch? Something told me IPR was much more than just an
institute for gifted children.

So much for the land of the free.

Even if I wanted to refuse, how could I now? If I did, then he'd expose my alter ego and I'd be sent away for sure to a whole *other* kind of institute. Forget my superhero days...My life was officially over!

---

"I CAN'T BELIEVE YOU'RE LEAVING. WHAT AM I SUPPOSED TO do without you?" My best friend Melody Stuart hugged me tight as we sat on my bed, her long auburn curls falling to her waist. "How are you supposed to function without your sidekick?"

"Trust me if I could pack you in my suitcase, I would," I answered sadly, "but the school is by invite only."

"What about Trevor? I heard he was going to ask you to the school dance."

My heart flipped like Donkey Kong, and I gave her a huge smile. "Really?"

"That's what Scott says. As Trevor's best friend, Scott should know."

My smile faded, and I sighed. "All the more reason for me to go. You know I can't date, especially someone I really like--like Trevor--because the hormone rush can short-circuit my system. I can't risk blocking any more 911 calls, or Digital Diva will be sent to the rescue and Blue Lake will be crawling with media again. Things are just getting back to normal for everyone. It's probably smart to lie low for a while, I guess."

"How long is a while?"

I shrugged. "No clue. Long enough to please my parents and give Trevor a chance to forget about me." Sadness filled me at that thought, but I had no choice. Life was so unfair sometimes.

"This stinks. You're going away. Your dad is moving back to L.A. and Simon is leaving to intern with him for a couple weeks, and Maria is a mess. Our core group is falling apart. If Scott breaks up with me, I'll go completely mental."

The doorbell rang, and my parents hollered that Agent Maxwell was here. It was time for me to go.

"Oh my God, your parents aren't even driving you?" Mel gaped at me.

"I know, right? Stupid Dark Shades Man convinced them it would be easier this way since I'm their only child. He offered to escort me, so now he's like their hero or something. If they only knew he has way more of an agenda on his mind than just my well being. I don't trust him one bit. And I don't even get to say goodbye to Trevor. He's really going to hate me now."

"I'll make sure he doesn't." Mel's voice hitched. "Man I'm gonna miss you."

"Me too." I hugged her again, then jumped up and grabbed my stuff. "I'll text you every day."

"You'd better." She sniffed, then wiped her eyes before following me out of my bedroom, backing me up like an automatic file on my hard drive. "Hurry back, okay?"

"Count on it," I whispered as we joined my parents and Dark Shades Man at the front door.

"Miss Granger." Agent Maxwell tipped his head, still wearing his annoying sunglasses and yet another dark suit.

I didn't say a word, just handed him my suitcases and turned to my parents.

"You made the right decision, honey." Mom nodded once, stiffly, and I could tell she was trying hard not to cry. She hated to show weakness of any kind. "We'll check in with you in a couple weeks. Give you time to settle in and get used to your new routine. But I still expect you to call me every day. Are you sure that new cell phone I gave you is working properly?"

Agent Maxwell's lips twitched.

"It's fine, Mom. I'll be fine, too." I nodded once, just like she had. The next thing I knew, she wrapped me in the tightest hug I think she's ever given me. "It won't be for long, honey, I promise," she whispered in my ear, and then stepped back looking calm and composed once more.

I turned to Dad and tears instantly flooded my eyes. He didn't say a word, just gave me a humongous bear hug. "You going to be okay, sweetie? You can always change your mind and stay here. No one can force you to do something you don't really want to. You know that, right?"

I paused, but then my gaze met that of Agent Maxwell, who slowly took off his sunglasses and raised a brow at me. I sighed, finished hugging Dad, and then stepped back.

"It's okay. I'm sad about leaving, but I've thought about what all of you said, and I agree. IPR sounds amazing. I'll just miss everyone."

"My brave girl." His eyes looked a little misty. "If you're sure...?"

"I'm sure." I glanced around. "Where's Gram? I can't leave without saying goodbye to her."

Gram appeared out of nowhere, all bundled up in her winter coat with suitcases trailing behind her. "If I've told you once, I've told you a million times--I go where you go." She shot me a wide smile, and I flew into her arms.

I grinned at Agent Maxwell's stunned face. "*Now* I'm ready."

"B-but, Gabby, you can't go," Mom stammered, looking flustered for the first time ever.

"It's a free country." Gram thrust her chin in the air.

"Mom, the Institute is for gifted students," Dad added.

"I'm gifted." Gram tapped her head. "Photographic memory, remember. Maybe I can help Sammy out while she's there. Be a tutor of sorts. At the very least, settle the poor girl in properly." She gave both my parents a disapproving stare.

Agent Maxwell cleared his throat, his stunned face completely masked now. "Mrs. Granger, I don't think--"

"It's Ms. Fontana-Granger, and I don't care what you or anyone else thinks. I go where my granddaughter goes. She needs me, and that's that. Now let's get a move on. Time's a wastin'."

"I'll give you a ride," Agent Maxwell said as he opened the front door, "but the Institute is for invited guests only. Have you given any thought to where you'll stay?"

"Oh, don't you worry about me." Gram poked him in the chest. "I've been taking care of myself since long before you were out of diapers, boy. I'll be just fine. Let's go, Sammy, before this crazy fool lets all the heat out of the house." She marched outside to the dark, four door sedan without another word and climbed in.

I smirked and fluttered my lashes at Dark Shades Man. He just narrowed his eyes, slipping his sunglasses firmly back in place as he ushered me out the door. Things were looking up. At least I had Gram with me. What a great surprise. I chewed my lip, admitting I was at least a little curious over what other surprises might be in store for me.

Maybe my life wasn't completely over after all.

## 2

---

## SURPRISE!

We arrived at IPR, and I could see the school was legit. The massive brick building stood impossibly high which made it look a little scary, but the sun was shining on a fresh new layer of fluffy white snow, softening the image a bit. It had to be a real school, I thought to myself, pushing down the uneasy feeling I'd had during the long car ride here. Students with backpacks were coming and going and actually smiling.

No armed guards or lab rats in sight.

I couldn't believe the students had to wear a uniform, but at least instead of the standard navy blue and gold, theirs was a cool turquoise and sparkly silver combo which looked kind of familiar. Turquoise blazers with IPR embroidered in silver on the lapel, silver pleated pants and skirts, and totally cute turquoise and silver plaid knee socks for the girls. Still...

"No one said anything about having to wear a uniform," I pointed out to Agent Maxwell.

"Dress codes inspire order and uniformity. This school

has an impressive reputation. You should feel lucky to have gotten an invitation."

"And just how do you know so much about this school?" Gram eyed Agent Maxwell critically.

He met her gaze point blank. "Because the FBI is one of IPR's biggest sponsors." At her pursed lips, he explained. "This school has produced some of our top agents as well as some of the most impressive people in the United States, from scientists to writers to politicians. You don't have to worry, Ms. Fontana-Granger. Your granddaughter is in good hands here."

He was telling the truth. I'd also googled the school's history on the way here, using my internal Internet. But that still hadn't squashed the niggling doubt lurking at the back of my brain. Something was off. I just wasn't sure what yet.

Gram harrumphed. "I'll be the judge of that soon enough." She jerked her head toward the doors. "Well, come on then. Let's get my granddaughter settled in."

"About that." Agent Maxwell blocked her path. "Miss Granger is a part of a select group of students chosen to test this new program. The school has left specific instructions for no outsiders to be allowed within the private wing set aside just for these students. In order for the results of this test study to be authentic, it is imperative the students be sequestered with no outside influences. It's in the contract."

And there it was, I thought.

"In the contract? What'd you use, microscopic print? No one said anything about locking my grandbaby up like some criminal." Gram grabbed my gloved hand. "Come on, Sammy, we're leaving."

I'd known in my gut we wouldn't be like the other students here, but I'd also known there was nothing I could do except ride the wave and see exactly what the government was up to. "Um, Gram, wait." I tugged her back and turned to Agent Maxwell. "Would it be all right if I talked to my grandmother alone for a minute?"

He studied me in silence, then walked several yards away.

"Sammy, you don't have to stay here," Gram said.

"Yes, I do." I told her about the Digital Diva costume I'd received--with the same color scheme as the IPR uniforms I now realized--and the text I'd gotten right after the showdown, and then seeing Agent Maxwell drive off. "The text was from the government. I'm sure it was him. He knows my secret. If I don't cooperate, he'll expose me for who I am. You know what will happen if the world finds out."

Gram growled in frustration. "You'll become some guinea pig." She shook her head. "It's just not right for the government to play hard ball like this. There has to be something we can do."

"It's okay. You're here if I need you, and they can't take my cell hand away so I can call you any time." I hugged her. "Besides, part of me wants to know what this class is all about and who these other mystery students are. Maybe the answer to reversing my uniqueness is inside those walls."

"Well now, I hadn't thought about that. I suppose checking it out wouldn't hurt. You just be on your guard." She leaned forward and tapped my nose. "Don't say too much, and keep your eyes open, you hear me?"

"Yes, ma'am." I saluted her and grinned.

"You call me day or night if you need anything. I'm staying with a friend of mine close by. Here's the number." She stuffed a piece of paper in my hand. I stared at it, dilating my retinas until I focused in with my camera eyes, then I blinked, taking a picture. The image zipped along the information highway of my brain via my sensory neurons, until it was stored in a file in the memory folds of my cerebrum.

I handed the paper back to her, blinking away the flash that still glowed behind my eyeballs. "Thanks, Gram. You're always there for me." I turned back to Agent Maxwell as he joined us once more. "I'm ready now."

"Good." He studied my shining eyes a little suspiciously, until Gram cleared her throat loudly. "It's been a pleasure, Ms. Fontana-Granger."

"Says you," Gram muttered.

He ignored her comment. "I'll have my driver take you wherever you'd like."

"So you can spy on me, too? No thanks. I'll find my own ride. Remember, Sammy, call if you need anything, and let me know when they give you a little time off for good behavior." She winked at me, scowled at Agent Maxwell, then marched down the street with her nose in the air.

Agent Maxwell grumbled beside me, "Now I know where you get your spunk from." Rubbing his temples, he led the way. "Follow me, Miss Granger, the welcome assembly's about to start."

———

WE SLIPPED INTO THE MASSIVE AUDITORIUM, AND I SAT IN THE back row. I hated sitting in the front, hated to be the center of attention.

Agent Maxwell could give a hoot. He glanced over his shoulder, frowned, and motioned for me to follow him. Reluctantly, I pushed myself to me feet and followed his lead to the front to join the small group of students in the first couple rows. There were five girls, five boys, and myself.

This school accommodated hundreds, so where was everyone else?

"I'll go get you registered and have your luggage taken to your dorm. *You* have a seat." He pointed to a spot right next to a boy about my age with a golden blond buzz cut and stormy gray eyes.

The boy looked pretty average...until he smiled up at me.

My heart literally skipped a beat like a skip on a DVD. He had full lips, perfectly straight teeth, and eyes that crinkled into the cutest dreamy expression. I'd never seen anything like it. How a simple smile could transform Mr. Ordinary into Mr. Adorable within seconds. Man oh man, I was in big trouble now.

His smile slipped a little and Mr. Ordinary returned, much to my relief. "You okay?" he asked.

"I'm fabulastic!" I squeaked, then cleared my throat and sat, looking straight ahead at the stage. Why did cute boys turn me into a tongue-tied goofball? I'd meant to say fabulous, changed my mind to fantastic, and out popped fabulastic.

"Fabulastic?" he asked, the amusement in his voice crystal clear.

"Yeah, it's all the rage where I come from."

"Guess it hasn't caught on in my area yet." He leaned in close and said in a soft husky voice, "I'm Brent Matthews by the way." He reached out his hand. "Want a piece of gum?" The smell of spearmint tickled my nose.

I shot him a quick glance, but that darn smile was back in place, and Mr. Adorable was present and accounted for. "I'm Samantha Granger, but you can call me Sam." I smiled back at him weakly, relieved I'd sounded normal as I helped myself to a stick of gum. "Thanks."

Up until now Trevor had been the only boy to make my

hormones skyrocket. The last thing I needed was to get close to another boy who might trigger my love meter. I just couldn't risk my fellow students finding out how "different" I was, so I popped the gum in my mouth, chewed slowly, and focused on the reason I was here.

To find a cure.

"So, Brent Matthews, do you know what this special class is all about?" I asked, still not looking at him. "I mean, there are only eleven of us. Where is everyone else?"

"Well, Fabulastic Sam, looks like we're about to find out." He pointed to the stage as a woman in a pin-striped suit and short cropped, stark white hair stepped up to the podium.

"Good afternoon, boys and girls. My name is Ms. Zimmerman, and I am your Headmistress. Standing to my left are your teachers. Mrs. Troubadour is a professor of Biology, Mr. Hillcrest is a professor of Chemistry, and Miss Westcott is a professor of physics. And finally, world renowned fusion expert, Dr. Guggenheim, will be joining us tomorrow."

I glanced at my fellow students and saw the same confusion I felt. What the heck kind of program were we involved in?

Headmistress Zimmerman continued. "You might all be wondering why only eleven of you have been chosen for this special interest class, and what all this science has to do with the program. Well, standing to my right is Special Agent Crawford of the FBI. I think it best if I let her explain." Headmistress Zimmerman stepped back, and Special Agent Crawford took her place.

"A few months ago a radioactive meteor fell from the sky," Special Agent Crawford said and stared us down one by one. Her long black hair and angelic face didn't match the tough look in her eyes.

Her words registered in my brain, and my heart started pounding like the bass on my iPod. She wasn't going to tell them about me, was she? Forget my fresh start; I'd go back to being a freak. I risked a peek at the boy beside me and was surprised to see beads of sweat popping out on his forehead. Mr. Ordinary looked as nervous as I felt, and I couldn't help wonder why.

"We thought there was only one of you." Her gaze locked onto mine for a brief moment, and I forgot to breathe, but then she started talking again. "What you don't know is that there wasn't just one meteor. A cosmic shower dropped radioactive meteors over various parts of the United States."

We all gasped and glanced at each other warily. Could it be? Was it possible I wasn't the only freak in Freaksville?

"That's right," Special Agent Crawford continued. "Each one of you is special in your own unique way, and we are here to help."

Panicked comments rumbled throughout the rows around me. One boy jumped to his feet, only to have another FBI agent firmly return him to his seat.

"Relax." Crawford's face changed from intimidating to reassuring faster than a broadband connection, reminding me of a chameleon. Except everyone knows that chameleons are sneaky.

"You're not lab rats or prisoners," she went on. "We only want to make sure you are not a threat to national security. We will help you all discover exactly what you are capable of, then teach you how to control your abilities so you will be able to function better in society.

You *will* be able to go home … in time. But for now you will be sequestered for your own good. We have hand selected and screened a special team to work with you, so everyone you come in contact with will know your situation. They are sworn to secrecy. You *will* be safe here, I promise."

"Thank you, Special Agent Crawford," Headmistress Zimmerman said and resumed her place in front of the podium. "I know this is a lot to take in; therefore, the rest of today will be spent getting you all settled in your dorms. Your suitcases have been stored in a safe place, as you will have no need for them at this time. We have provided you with everything. You will be expected to wear the uniforms hanging in your closets at all times unless otherwise instructed. Your professors will explain why when your lessons begin."

More grumbling echoed around me, especially from the girls.

"Classes will start tomorrow morning at eight A.M. sharp. I'm sure many of you have questions, and they will be answered in due time, but for now I suggest you all follow Special Agent Crawford to the elevator in the back. A private wing has been created in the basement. Remember, you are not allowed to leave at any time. When you enrolled in this class, you entered into a binding contract. Any violators will be severely punished."

She leaned forward, looking intimidating. "Believe me when I say you don't want to test me ... or you *will* pay a price." She paused for one long tense moment, and then finished with, "You have been dismissed."

I stood up, afraid to say a word, totally shocked over what I'd just heard. Sequestered in a basement, not allowed to leave, special uniforms required, tests and training...We really were imprisoned lab rats!

I was finding out the government never did anything without a reason. They might say they were holding us here for our own safety. That they were only trying to help us. But I knew better.

They wanted something from us.

I didn't have a clue what it was, and I'd be lying if I said I wasn't worried, but I vowed right then and there ... I wouldn't rest until I figured out what it was. My stomach turned like my automatic CD cleaner, and I actually felt sick. I had a feeling this adventure would take me to a whole new level.

What on earth had I gotten myself into this time?

# 3

# THE OTHERS

"Okay, people, this is it. Welcome to your new home," Special Agent Crawford said as we stepped off the elevator, her long black hair falling down her back like a waterfall of silk. She looked like an angel, but I doubted there was an angelic bone in her body.

"At one end of the floor you'll see the boys' wing, and at the other end you'll see the girls' wing," she went on. "Each suite has three bedrooms and one bathroom. You will find your name and that of your roommate's on the door to the bedroom you will be staying in. Boys are not allowed in the girls' suite, and girls are not allowed in the boys' suite." She turned to us with a penetrating, meaningful stare. "Do I make myself clear?"

We all nodded hard, no one daring to speak still.

"Good." She turned back around and continued forward. "Out in the center, there is a common room for all the students to hang out and get to know each other. There are no TV's or radios so you will have no connection to the outside world, and everything you do will be monitored and screened." She looked right at me, stared for a second, then looked at everyone else.

The warning was clear: don't try anything foolish, or you're toast.

"We do, however, have pool, Ping Pong, cards, and video games to keep you busy. As well as a small gym for exercise and a mini-kitchen filled with snacks in case you get hungry. Any questions?"

We just looked around at each other.

"Adult advisors will be popping in at any given moment, so we will know if anyone is breaking the rules. And we have two upperclassmen RA's who will be living here with you full time. They graduate this year and will be interning with your professors, so they are fully aware of your situation. Lance Anderson and Tracy Robbins will be available if you have any questions or just need to talk. Well, that about does it for me. I'll take your cell phones now."

She held out her hand, and we all complied without as much as a groan. We didn't dare.

"Good luck," she said and turned on her heel, disappearing inside the elevator.

Everyone stared at each other for only a second and then bolted into the center common room. Boys and girls split off to their separate wings to check out their rooms and find out who their roommates were.

Everyone except me.

I ran the opposite way, straight to the elevator. I didn't dare call Gram, knowing someone somewhere would hear every word and turn me in. Feeling completely cut off and alone, I searched the elevator for floor numbers, hoping this was all a dream. But there weren't any numbers.

I'd made a huge mistake in coming here!

I pulled off my glove and touched my cell hand. My palm turned a transparent glowing blue-green, and below that my flesh colored bumps raised up. There had to be something I could do to help myself escape.

"Don't even think about it, kid," said a female voice from behind me.

Yanking on my glove, I whirled around and gaped, the blood draining from my face faster than the battery on my PSP.

"And don't bother with the elevator," she went on. "It won't open, you know. Besides, they have hidden cameras and are watching every move you make. Not to mention they can intercept and block any call before the connection even goes through. It's Big Brother here, big time. You may as well accept your fate and get with the program."

I wilted in relief. It wasn't Special Agent Crawford. This girl had to be my new RA, Tracy Robbins. She looked older and stood almost six feet tall with her arms crossed in front of her and a scowl on her chiseled, Amazon-like face. She might be even scarier than Special Agent Crawford.

"I was just--"

"Save it." She swiped her hand through the air, glaring daggers at me. "I don't care about your excuses. Just follow the rules, or you'll have to deal with me. I thought I would be involved with the test program when I signed up for this, but no, I get stuck baby-sitting you brats. I *hate* baby-sitting!"

"But I'm not a--"

"Look, quit trying to escape, and we'll get along just fine. You can start by meeting your roommate and unpacking your junk." She turned around and marched off to the girls' suite where some kind of argument had broken out. "Knock it off, nimrods, or some heads are gonna roll," she shouted as she rounded the corner.

"Great." I let out a breath and followed Warden Robbins to my cell as slow as a netbook without enough memory. I didn't care what anyone said, this place was definitely a prison. Only one problem.

I'd never done well in confined spaces.

---

I STARED UP AT A DOOR WITH MY NAME ON IT AND READ THE name of the other girl out loud. "Francesca Ferrari."

"That's me," said a voice from inside the room. "I'm guessing you're Samantha Granger?"

I walked in the rest of the way and answered her smile with one of my own. Francesca had long, curly auburn hair and pretty amber eyes. Kind of like Mel, yet so not. Perfect clothes, perfect makeup, perfect figure, perfect everything. I stifled a groan. Just...perfect. "Yup. Guess we're roommates."

"Super," she said in a perfectly peppy cheerleader voice. "Hope you don't mind, but I snagged the bed on the right."

"Sure, that's fine." I sat on my bed and looked around, deciding she seemed nice enough. "We don't even have a window?" I scrunched my eyebrows together.

"Guess they figured we might escape after finding out what this program is really like." She rolled her eyes.

"Yeah, no kidding. Like any of us would have signed up if we'd known we were going to be prisoners."

"Wait until you open your closet. They can't seriously expect us to wear the same clothes every day. I mean that is *so* boring."

"I'm almost afraid to find out." I walked to my closet, grabbed the doorknob, then peeked inside. Hanging there was the same sparkly silver jumpsuit with Digital Diva embroidered across the front in turquoise that Agent Maxwell had left on my doorstep. But it wasn't alone. There were seven in all. One for every day of the week.

"This has to be a joke."

"Oh, it's no joke." Francesca opened her closet and pulled out an identical jumpsuit, except the name on hers was 'Fashionista.'

"Fashionista?" I asked, looking her over curiously.

A twinkle glittered in her eyes seconds before she blinked them, changing her green eye shadow to purple instantly.

My mouth fell open. "That's amazing. What else can you do?"

She giggled. "Well, lots actually. Watch this." She shook her hair and blonde highlights streaked through her auburn waves. Next she pressed her lips together and changed the shade of her lip gloss from peach to pink. "I can do all kinds of fashion and style stuff, but it makes me tired and gives me some pretty weird side effects. How about you?"

"Same here. I get totally tired out, and yeah, all kinds of weird stuff happens to me after I use my powers. Not easy to explain why my nails and eyelashes are so much longer literally overnight. I've had to trim them a ton. And don't get me started on my eyebrows. I can go from pencil thin to bushy caterpillars within an hour."

"I know, right?" She laughed, then studied me. "So...what *can* you do, anyway?"

This might be a prison, but it suddenly hit me. Serving my sentence might not be so bad. I didn't have to hide here, and I wasn't alone. I could make friends. I could say or do anything.

Maybe I could even date!

It didn't matter if my internal pressure cooker bubbled over completely. If the government could intercept my phone calls, for sure they could stop me from blocking a 911 call. My heart swelled like the speakers on my boom box as a certain Mr. Adorable flashed into my mind, stealing my breath for a second. Maybe one totally cute Brent Matthews was exactly what I needed to forget about Trevor Hamilton once and for all.

I bit my lip and pulled off my glove, tapping my hand and bringing the transparent, blue-green veiny screen to life. I showed Francesca. "I'm Digital Diva. I come equipped with a cell phone in my hand, GPS in my head, camera in my eyes, and full Internet capabilities." I left off the part about having a military weapon inside me, not wanting to be over the top. "But I'm sure my Powers aren't as much fun as yours must be."

"Are you kidding?" She stared at me in awe. "I can just change my clothes, hair, and makeup. Your powers are awesome. I'd love to have all that technology at my fingertips."

"It's pretty cool, I guess." An unexpected wave of pride washed over my system like a screensaver. I never thought I'd say something positive about what had happened to me. I still didn't want to be like this forever, but being around other unique people like me somehow made it easier to accept.

"Come on. Let's go meet the other girls." Francesca grabbed my arm and pulled me with her out into the hall.

Our bedroom was the first room, closest to the bathroom. The bedroom across the hall had 'Gi Wong' and 'Hope O'Reilly' written on the door. Peeking inside we saw a girl with jet-black hair, dark eyes, and piercings arguing with another girl who wore no makeup and had a short blond pixie cut.

"I hate guns," said the pixie.

"Yeah, well I hate chores. You're not my mother, so quit trying to make me do them." The spiky-haired girl, who had to be Gi, wore a furious expression.

"Then quit being a slob," the pixie, who must be Hope, shot back.

"You want to see a real mess, I'll give you one." Gi squeezed her fists. One hand transformed into air-soft gun and the other into a paintball gun. She took aim, blasting Hope's side of the room with plastic BB pellets and paint.

Hope squealed and hopped onto her bed in seconds. "You're impossible." She spit a stream of blue cleaning fluid onto the wall and used her sponge-like palms to scrub off the paint before it could dry.

"Maybe we should meet the other girls first," I whispered to Francesca as the battle played out before us.

"I think you're right," she whispered back, and we tiptoed down the hall to the last bedroom. This room had 'Michaela Delgado' and 'Amy Newlander' written on the door. We were about to knock when the door flew open and a tall, athletic-looking girl with dark blond hair and fire in her green eyes stormed out.

She yelled, "Sports are not dumb. At least I do something useful with my time, you deflated ballhead."

A shorter girl with silky smooth, dark brown hair and brown eyes ran out after her, shouting back, "The name's Michaela, you wingnut. I know how to fix things. All you can do is kick a stupid ball around."

The girl who had to be Amy whirled around. "Stupid ball? I'll show you who's stupid." She turned her stomach to

Jell-O, reached in and grabbed a soccer ball, and then kicked it straight at Michaela's head.

Michaela just laughed as she transformed her arm into a chainsaw and sliced the ball in half in mid-air. "Fix that, hot rod." She slammed the door behind her. Amy shrieked and ran into the bathroom.

"I'm so glad I have you for a roommate," I said to Francesca as we stood in the empty hall alone and stunned.

"I know. They're all crazy. Hopefully the boys are more normal." Her lips curled up all catlike. "Or at least the cute one with the buzz cut."

"You mean Brent?" I asked, a weird feeling hitting the pit of my stomach. Something told me she'd seen Mr. Adorable's smile, too.

"Yeah, that's the one. I know you sat next to him and everything, but I met him first. That means I get first dibs. Sorry." She shrugged with a bubbly smile like she hadn't just dropped a bomb on my plans to forget about Trevor. "In fact, I think I'll go talk to Brent now. I wonder what his powers are," she said all dreamy-like.

"B-But we're not supposed to go into the boys' suite," I sputtered desperately. Anything to keep her from going to him. There was no way I could compete with someone who looked like a cover model.

"We might not be able to go in, silly, but that doesn't mean I can't get him to come out. My power of persuasion has always been one of my strengths. Just ask my parents." She marched off down the hall without a backward glance, not even asking me to join her. "Cover for me, would ya?" was the only thing she said as she sailed through our suite doors into the common room.

I didn't feel so lucky now.

The bedroom door at the far end of the hall flew open

wide, and Warden Robbins stormed out. "Who is making all the noise out here?" She glared down the hall, hands on her hips, obviously annoyed. And then her gaze landed on me.

Uh-oh.

Forget annoyance; her eyes turned stone hard.

"Granger, my room--now!"

## 4

### INTRO TO FUSION

The next morning, after spending the night in solitary confinement, I spent an hour scrubbing the toilets with a toothbrush for something I didn't even do. Besides, we have a cleaning lady who comes once a week!

It really wasn't fair. I didn't sneak out, and I wasn't the one who made all the noise. But Warden Robbins wouldn't let me explain. I marched out of the bathroom to an empty suite.

Doors were open and rooms were vacant, except for Warden Robbins. No way did I want to get stuck alone with her. She had it in for me for some reason. My cranky suitemates were definitely the lesser of two evils. Not to mention, I was now late for class, thank you very much.

Not the kind of first impression I wanted to give my teachers.

I quickly changed into my school uniform, which was not like the rest of the school's. These suckers molded to our bodies like a second layer of skin, leaving *nothing* to the imagination. I wasn't used to wearing my disguise without a mask, but given that we were prisoners and all, I guess it didn't really matter. It wasn't like we were going anywhere.

Still...

Searching the room for something, anything, I grabbed a notebook and held it in front of my chest, feeling totally exposed. Hurrying down the hall past the common room to the elevators, I stopped before the open doors. I stepped inside, and they closed eerily behind me as though a ghost was operating the machine. There were no buttons to push, yet the elevator moved like it knew exactly where it was supposed to go.

The doors opened on a floor with a long hallway and several rooms that looked like lab rooms. That uneasy feeling I'd had since learning about this place returned in full force. Mumbled conversations sounded from down the hall, so I followed the noise to an open classroom.

"There you are," Francesca said, waving me over from her spot in the back row by Brent. "I didn't think you'd ever get here." She pointed to a chair beside her, far away from him.

Everyone stopped talking and all eyes fixed on me, sizing me up and making me squirm. I really did hate being the center of attention. I quickly sat and hoped I'd stop blushing. Brent smiled at me. Mr. Adorable was so not helping matters in the cooling-of-the-cheeks department.

I looked anywhere but into his dreamy eyes. "Hi," I squeaked with a quick wave. Most of the girls waved back, a few of the guys nodded, and one boy who was almost too pretty to be real gave me a smirk.

"Now that everyone is here, why don't we get started," said a tall man with a funny accent, thick black hair--kind of like one of my mom's throw rugs--and super thick glasses. "My name is Dr. Guggenheim, and I am a fusion expert.

These are my esteemed colleagues whom you all met yester-day. Professor Troubadour, Hillcrest, and Westcott. Let me start by saying how honored and excited we all are to take part in this study--"

"Program, Doctor, program," Professor Troubadour said. She gave us a wink and a reassuring smile. "This is all new to these students, and we don't want to alarm them in any way."

The doctor stared blankly at the professor for a moment and then chuckled. "Silly me. Of course I meant 'program.' Being an expert scientist rather than a professor, I'm simply used to referring to everything as a study."

He adjusted his glasses and smiled kindly at us. "Rest assured, boys and girls, you are in very capable hands. We are simply here to help you figure out exactly what you're capable of and then teach you how to reach your full potential."

"Then, dude, why do we have to wear these lame outfits?" A boy with long, purple-streaked red hair tugged at the skintight unitard. "I feel like a ballerina. Gotta say, it's not working for me, bro." A few snickers came from around the room.

"Well," Dr. Guggenheim paused, turned to Professor Hillcrest, and said, "I don't want to hog the spotlight. Why don't I let the good professor fill you in since his team of chemists designed the uniforms."

"Absolutely, Doctor." Professor Hillcrest faced us. "You all have gone through something remarkable, making you special. Since the government was able to track you, we designed these suits to protect you. The fibers in this mate-rial will block anyone on the outside from being able to track you. This material can withstand extreme tempera-tures and is fire retardant. In addition, virtually nothing can pierce it. You will be safe here while we test and teach you the skills you'll need to function as normally as possible in society."

"Thank you, Professor," the doctor said. "The floor is yours, boys and girls. How about we start with you, ladies, followed by the gents? Enlighten us with your own unique stories. That way we're on the same page, and there will be no surprises." Dr. Guggenheim turned to his colleagues. "Professors, please observe and take notes. We will discuss and evaluate after class."

The professors stepped to the sides of the room to quietly observe, but we all just sat there. Everyone looked at each other, then all eyes turned to me. No way was I going first.

On a huff of frustration, my roommate stood up and strolled to the front like a model working a runway. She stopped, pointed her toe, and then pivoted perfectly, totally rocking her unitard.

I repeat: life was so unfair.

"Hi guys." She tossed her long auburn curls and smiled at Brent. "The name's Francesca Ferrari, but you can call me Fashionista."

"Fashion-whata?" someone asked.

"You know--clothes, hair, makeup." Everyone stared at her in confusion, so she fluttered her lashes, changing her eye shadow from brown to purple with matching lowlights in her hair. "So, like, I was home alone and getting ready to go to a party, when a meteor crashed into our house. Now I come fully equipped with all the supplies I need to style and change my hair color and makeup anywhere I am. Pretty cool, huh?"

"Dudette, that's pretty lame if you ask me," said the red-haired boy in the front. "Don't get me wrong. I like the idea of changing my hair color whenever I want, but it's not very scary. What are you going to do--tease me to death?" He laughed at his joke.

Francesca just tucked her hair behind her ear and then blasted his butt clear to the back of the room with her blow-dryer ear. "Is that scary enough for you, *dude?*" He didn't utter as much as a peep. Rubbing her hands together, she strolled back to her seat with a smug smile on her perfect face. "Top that, people."

Gi Wong stomped to the front of the room without hesitation. "Fashionista? *Puh-lease*," she said as she faced us, proudly showing off the name 'Gunner Girl.' "I was in the middle of an all-out war in my back yard with my friends when I tripped over a meteorite. Watch this." She wagged her eyebrows and goggle shields popped out, covering her eyes. Next, she shook her shoulders, and a vest covered her upper torso. Making a gun with her pointer finger and thumb, she took aim and pelted a poster in the back of the room with air-soft pellets to form the letter G. Then made an exclamation mark beside it with black paint balls shooting out the pointer finger on her other hand.

"You have friends?" Her roommate fluttered her eyelashes, staring up at her all innocent-like.

Gi smirked and then hit her dead center in the forehead with a Nerf dart that shot out of her pinkie. Gi blew on her little finger as though blowing away smoke and smirked. "You asked for it, roomy." She made the peace sign and took her seat.

Hope O'Reilly gasped, grabbing the dart off her face. She hopped to her feet, rushed to the back of the room, showered the wall with a stream of neon-orange cleaning solution, and scrubbed the poster with her Brillo-pad palms. After quickly taping the poster back together with tape from her fingertip dispenser, she turned, glanced at the window, and tsked.

A threaded needle sprouted out of another one of her fingers, and she proceeded to rapidly stitch a ripped corner of the curtain. She smoothed her apron-covered unitard and walked to the front of the room with her head held high.

Facing us, she said, "Forgive my roommate. She's a slob. I, on the other hand, am not. Home-Ec Helper is my name. I clean my mom's friends' houses in my neighborhood for money on the side."

"Home-Wreck Helper is more like it," Gi scoffed.

"Um, wrecking homes would be your department. Cleaning up after you seems to be mine." Hope straightened the hem of her apron. "Anyhow, where was I? Oh, that's right. A meteorite hit the house I was cleaning, and well, I guess you've pretty much seen what I can do. Add baking to the mix, and that's my story." She shrugged and then took her seat far away from her "roomy." "I'm excited to be here, just not thrilled about rooming with her."

"Trade ya." The jockette with the super-long legs jogged to the front of the room, her toned body flexing with every step. She turned to us. "The name's Amy Newlander, and the nickname's Athletica."

"More like Athletic Cup," her roommate grumbled.

"Funny, Grease Monkey, but I'm in the spotlight now, so can it. In fact, I was in the spotlight when all this meteor stuff went down. I'd just been chosen as MVP, so I was out back of our school in the equipment shed getting ready to practice soccer when out of nowhere a meteorite struck the shed." She beamed. "Now I'm in the spotlight with every sport."

The pretty boy in the front of the room snorted. "That'll be the day a girl can outplay a boy."

"Yeah?" Amy's stomach turned into a watery Jell-O mold, revealing a bottomless pit of equipment ready and waiting. "Name the time, the place, and the game. I'll school your butt any day of the week."

"Next," one of the professors quickly said.

Amy glared at the boy and then jogged back to her seat.

"Guess that leaves me, Michaela Delgado," said the dark-haired girl before me. She strode up front like she was used to taking charge. "Name's Mechanica, and I run my uncle's garage. I was rebuilding an old mustang when the meteorite destroyed the place. Now I don't need a garage at all since there isn't a piece of equipment I don't come equipped with." She shot Pretty Boy a scathing look. "And I know how to use every one." Her hand transformed into a blowtorch. "Care to test me, Ratchet Face?"

Pretty Boy squirmed, and Michaela locked eyes with Amy who grinned on a nod as though an alliance had been formed. Girls could pick on each other, but no way would we let any boy one-up us.

"Okay, Miss Granger, you're up." Dr. Guggenheim checked off my name as he stared down at his clipboard.

Goosbumps warped over my skin like a virus spreading through a computer. I'd really hoped they had forgotten about me. Having no choice, I lowered my notebook to my desk and decided to just get this craziness over with. Walking to the front of the room, I took a deep breath and then turned around and faced the class.

"Hi. My name is Samantha Granger, aka Digital Diva."

Someone went into a coughing fit on the side of the room, but I wasn't sure who. Even though our teachers had all been debriefed, they still looked shocked over witnessing our powers first hand. Maybe now they'd understand

exactly how freaked out we'd felt at discovering we had
powers in the first place.

"Hey, wait a minute. How come you're the only one
whose nickname doesn't start with the same letter as your
real name?" someone asked?

"Because I didn't think of that when I came up with the
nickname," I answered, looking at the surprised faces
staring back at me.

"You came up with your own nickname?" someone else
asked.

"Well, yeah, didn't you guys?" Ten heads shook back and
forth slowly, and I started to fidget.

"That's because Miss Granger is the only real superhero
among you." Doctor Guggenheim broke the silence.

"That's right," Professor Westcott said, referring to her
notes. "Sam is the first of your kind, and the only one to
draw national media attention. She was forced to become
a superhero, so she had no choice except to come up with
an alias and disguise. This is what led to our search for
others and discovery of the rest of you. When we created
your nicknames, we decided to match the letters to your
real names so it would be easier to remember your
powers."

"You mean we're superheroes, too?" another student
asked.

"Not yet, but you will be." Professor Hillcrest winked.
"By the time we're through with you, you'll be known as the
Phenoteens, an elite group of superheroes, saving the world
one mission at a time. With Digital Diva as you're your team
leader, of course."

I closed my eyes in dread. I had known the government
had some kind of secret plan for us; I just hadn't expected to
be the leader of anything. These kids all thought being a

superhero sounded glamorous and exciting. They had no idea what it was really like. I wanted no part of it.

My dad's words came back to me--No one could force me to do something I didn't want to. I'd be darned if I'd let them force me to be a superhero again, but I knew getting out of that wouldn't be as easy as just saying no.

I needed a plan.

Everyone stared at me like I had three heads. Great. Even under this crazy circus tent, I was still the number-one freak.

Professor Troubadour urged me on quietly with, "Proceed, child."

"Well, I was walking through the woods when I saw this glowing object. I had no idea it was a radioactive meteorite, or I never would have touched the thing. Anyway, I was holding my cell phone at the same time, and well, it sort of fused to my insides, I guess. So now I'm like a walking, breathing piece of technology."

"What does that mean?" someone asked.

"Can anyone say talk to the hand?" I giggled nervously as I pulled off my glove and showed them my glowing palm, but they just stared at me like they weren't impressed. "I...um...also have a GPS in my head, a camera in my eyes, and full Internet capabilities," I blurted, not wanting to look like a loser. "See." I pressed my temples and shot a holograph projection out of my eyes, displaying the main menu of my Electro Wave in a transparent screen before us.

It highlighted *everything* I could do.

All eyes widened as big as camcorder discs, and the professors' noises of astonishment echoed louder. Was that good or bad? I just didn't know anymore. I blinked, shutting down the holograph, but little rays of light lingered in my pupils, taking forever to fade away.

I rambled on even faster. "I have some military weapon apps that are pretty freaky, but I'm sure I'll be demonstrating those in lab, right?" I faced my professors and tried to breathe slowly so I wouldn't set off any alarms in the building. I needed to sit, like *now,* but they still just gaped at me. "Am I done?"

"Sure thing, Miss Granger. Thank you for sharing," Professor Westcott said, gathering her composure and looking at the other teachers in awe.

And then the bell rang.

"Okay, boys and girls. I'd say that's enough excitement for the morning," Doctor Guggenheim stammered, looking poleaxed and excited at the same time. "Why don't we break for lunch, and we will resume in the afternoon with the boys. I for one can't wait to see what they have in store for us."

I glanced at Brent and couldn't help but wonder if he still liked me. Never having imagined these words would cross my mind, I prayed, *Please, God, make him as much of a freak as I am.*

# 5
---
## FUSION 101

The glamour of being a superhero must have worn off, because we all eyed each other with uneasiness as we filed into the elevator. Phenoteens? Saving the world one mission at a time? This whole thing was crazy. What did the government expect us to do for them? Would we ever get to go home? Have normal lives? No one said a word as we waited to see where the mysterious contraption would take us this time.

The elevator lurched to a stop. The bell dinged, and the doors opened. Only, we weren't in our private wing. We were on the main level of the school, the halls loaded with students wandering about. My gaze shot to the others, and I could tell they were thinking the same thoughts I was.

*Freedom!*

This was our chance to escape. "Let's do this," I said, and walked through the elevator doors first.

"Let's do what, Miss Granger?" Special Agent Crawford moved in front of me, blocking my path.

"Um, let's do lunch?" I answered in question format on a hysterical giggle.

"That's what I thought you meant." Even though her eyes were covered with her own pair of dark shades, I knew they were staring at me. "Because if you meant anything else, that would give me grounds to take action. And trust me, nothing would give me more pleasure."

Chills zipped up my spine, and my internal alarms wailed in my inner ear.

She turned to the others. "We have an image to maintain here at IPR. We wouldn't want the public to think we were holding you here against your will, which we all know isn't the case--don't we?"

We nodded. Like we could do anything else.

"By enrolling in the test program, you all agreed to abide by the terms which include no communication with the outside world. The students here are aware of the test program, but they don't know the nature of the tests or about your abilities, which I trust you wish to keep a secret as much as we do."

She had us there, and she knew it.

"However, people do need to see we are clothing and feeding you, not harming you in any way. Therefore, you will be dining in the main dining room on a daily basis. You simply will not be allowed to speak with any of the other students. Is that clear?"

We nodded again.

"Good. Then follow me. A special table has been reserved for our class right up front." She turned and led the way while we trailed along behind her like the imprisoned lab rats we were, no matter what she said.

Wait a minute. We weren't wearing masks. The other kids might not be superheroes yet, but I was. What if someone recognized me from the news reports? I glanced down to see that my superhero name wasn't on my unitard anymore. The IPR logo embroidered in turquoise was in its place. The same was true for the other kids.

The government really *had* thought of everything.

Like a magic decoder ring, the special lighting in our prison wing revealed our superhero names. But out in public, we wore the same IPR emblem as every other student. I looked back up to find Special Agent Crawford giving me a knowing look. The invisible hand cuffs tightened around my wrists. I let out a sigh and followed in silence.

The hum of conversations, clatter of silverware against dishes, and movement in general came to a halt as we marched single file into the cafeteria. Our uniforms might be the same color scheme, but we so did not look like the other students. I'd never felt more exposed in my life--or more like the biggest doofus ever.

We quickly snatched our trays from the lunch line and took our seats. Meanwhile, Special Agent Crawford stood close by with a watchful eye as she talked to the cafeteria lady whose name badge read Alice Little.

Only Alice was anything but little. She looked like she'd swallowed the StayPuft Marshmallow Man whole! But she'd been super-bubbly and friendly as we went through the lunch line. But now, talking to Special Agent Crawford now, Alice gestured wildly with her hands like Gram did when she was upset about something.

"Hey, Fabulastic Sam, is this seat taken?" Brent asked as he sat down directly across from me. He smiled, erasing all thoughts of the flustered lunch lady from my brain.

"Fabsolutely," I answered.

"Let me guess. 'Fabsolutely' is all the rage where you come from, too?" He arched a brow, studying me.

"Fraid not." I shrugged, feeling like such a dork. "That's

just me trying to be funny but failing frightfully." *Mental forehead smack. Shut up now, Sam.*

He chuckled. "Cute."

My gaze met his. "Yeah?"

"Yeah." He smiled slowly and fully, his eyes crinkling in such an adorable way. I let out a long sigh that pretty much said exactly how I felt--deliciously dreamy.

"Are you all right?" he asked me, sounding concerned and looking totally ordinary once more. "You've got that weird look on your face again."

I rubbed the stars from my eyes and sat up straight, focusing on my lunch. "It's all good."

"What's all good?" Francesca chirped as she plunked down beside me, eyeing us both. Every girl knew when a friend called first dibs, that meant hands off--no matter how much you wanted to put your hands on.

I stifled my groan and smiled up at her. "The food." I gestured to my tray. "It's all good."

"Fabulous," Francesca said. "I'm starved."

"Fabulastic," Brent added.

"Huh?" Francesca peeked up at him, looking confused.

"I said that's fantastic." His gaze shot to mine, and he gave me a wink that I felt straight to my soul.

"Fantastic." Francesca's gaze locked on mine. "Kind of like being a *real* superhero which you never said anything about to your own roommate, Digital Diva." She sounded annoyed and wounded at the same time.

"Well, I, um--"

"Will fill us in later, right?" Brent jumped to my defense.

"Right," I responded in relief.

"That's what I figured." He grinned. "In the meantime, I'm starved. Let's eat."

"All right, troops, let's go." Special Agent Crawford joined us shortly, looking at her watch. "Time to get back to more important matters than food, like the rest of the introductions." She stared at our table. "Get ready, Matthews. You're up first."

Brent's Adam's apple bobbed. He'd only taken a bite when he dropped his fork. Guess he didn't like the spotlight any more than I did. "Great," was all he said, no smile in sight.

At least with Mr. Ordinary around, I stood a chance of making it through the rest of the day without breaking my word to my roommate. Brent Matthews was off limits. Maybe if I chanted that enough times in my mind, I'd start to believe it and stop drooling every time he was near. That drooling could be really inconvenient, considering that we lived on the same floor.

I swallowed hard and amended my prayer. *Forget making him "as" freaky as I am, God. I need him to be way freakier.* Because what I needed the most right now was a friend, and Francesca was the closest thing I had to that in this place. No matter how strong the temptation, friends didn't break their word.

"OKAY, MR. MATTHEWS, WE'RE READY WHENEVER YOU ARE," Dr. Guggenheim said, looking like an alarm clock wound way too tight.

I knew exactly how he felt. I held my breath, waiting for Brent to speak.

Brent stood at the front of the room just staring at us. Like he still wasn't sure it was okay to show us all what he could do. I could relate. For so long, we'd all felt we were the only one of our kind. To find out there were others was exciting and scary and just plain crazy.

His eyes met mine for a second, and I gave him a small smile and a nod. Francesca nailed me with a sharp glance, but I justified my gesture as being encouraging, not flirting. That was the truth. It was hard for any of us to put ourselves out there without the fear of something bad happening.

Brent took a shaky breath and started talking. "My name is Brent Matthews, and I am Boy-X."

"Like Xbox only Boy-X, as in video games?" Gi asked and Brent nodded. She reloaded her airsoft BB pellets and paint-ball fingers as she responded, "Coolio, Buckshot."

"So, what's your story, anyway?" Francesca leaned forward, resting her chin on her hands. She looked up at Brent through amazingly thick lashes as the most gorgeous pink highlights streaked through her long auburn strands of hair.

"Wh-what was the question," he stammered, blinking at her as though just now noticing how beautiful she was.

"Your story, dude. How you became radical like us," the boy with purple-streaked hair butted in, holding his hands up as if to say, *Come on already, man. Pick up the pace.*

"Oh, right." Brent wiped his palms on his thighs since his skintight unitard--which looked oh so hot on him--didn't have pockets to shove them into. "Well, I was in my base-ment in the middle of an Xbox Live tournament. The next thing I knew, a meteorite had crashed through both stories of my house and smashed my TV into a million pieces. And, well, now I can do this."

He shook out his hands then clasped them in front of him. Before our very eyes, his fingers fused together into an Xbox controller. The only free moving parts were his thumbs. "I have a built-in headset so I can talk to and play anyone who's on Xbox Live. And whatever game I'm playing, I can transfer the things I win into the actual room where I am at the time. Watch."

He played a quick game of something that looked like it was easy for him as he explained, "If I win so many battles or races or whatever and earn so many points, I can buy new things like cars and other cool stuff, see?" A brand-new, candy-apple-red sports car appeared in the center of the room. "Game on!" He spread his arms wide, staring proudly at the car before him.

The girls oohed and ahhed, while the boys hooted and hollered.

Brent stood a little straighter, and a crooked grin formed on his full lips. "Whatever objects I put in the room I can move and control with my hands." He hit another button, and the car roared to life.

"Mr. Matthews--" all of our professors spoke at once.

"Sorry." He shrugged, not looking sorry at all. Then he hit another button, and the car disappeared. He took his seat with a lot more confidence than when he'd left.

"Guess I'll go next since I'm Boy-X's roommate." A short, stocky boy with thin, dark hair parted on the side and pale-blue watery eyes made his way to the front of the room and faced us.

"My name is Parker Schofield, but I'm better known as Picasso Kid. My parents rented out an art studio for me, and I was working late on my biggest project ever when the meteorite hit."

"Ohhh, I love art," Hope said, giving Parker a friendly smile. "So what do you do? Draw, paint, sketch?"

He flushed slightly under her praise. "All of the above." He held out one palm, which transformed into a pallet, and then he spread the fingers on his other hand wide. Just as with Wolverine from X-Men, objects sliced through the boy's fingertips. Only these objects weren't knives; they were a pen, pencil, chalk and paint brush.

"I also have a canvas on my stomach. If I create an image, my stomach glows internally and the image is projected and burned onto any surface I aim at." He lifted his shirt, and his stomach started to quiver.

"We'll take your word for it, son. After Mr. Matthews's little display, I think we'll all wait until Lab to show our demonstrations," Dr. Guggenheim quickly said. "Next?"

Parker shot a disappointed glance in Hope's direction and then lowered his shirt and returned to his seat.

"Dude, I'll totally go next." The boy with purple-streaked red hair and honey eyes ran and slid across the floor and then pivoted on his heel when he hit the front of the room. "The name's Warren Thompson, but you can call me Wheels."

"Big surprise there," Michaela said, changing her fingers into various tools and looking bored. "Let me guess, you were roller-skating when you had your close encounter."

"No way, dudette. I was on my way to practice roller*blading*. Big difference," he said, and she just rolled her eyes. "So, like I was riding my BMX bike. My pack was full with my skateboard and my blades when I took a jump and totally landed on this weird-looking rock. Freaked me out big time, but it gave me mad skills, so I'm not complaining. Watch and learn, my people."

One of our professors opened her mouth to speak, but Warren didn't give her a chance. He let out a whoop as actual wheels of various sizes popped out of his hands and feet. A helmet slid out from under his hairline to cover his head, and knee and elbow pads popped out of his joints. He took off like a shot, zipping around the room and jumping over our heads at warp speed.

"Mr. Thompson, I said that's enough. Save it for lab," Dr. Guggenheim shouted, finally getting through to the boy.

Warren hit the brakes and skidded to a stop, tires screeching loudly across the floor. "Sorry, dude. Sometimes I get carried away." He adjusted his body, and his gear disappeared as quickly as it had popped out. He slid back to his seat, wagging his brows at Michaela all the way.

The doctor just shook his head and glanced at his clipboard. "Three down, two to go." He looked up. "Who's next?"

A boy with creamy milk-chocolate-colored skin, an impressive Afro, and pale-green eyes stared at Pretty Boy. But Pretty Boy made a face at him and refused to budge.

The boy grumbled, "No wonder they gave you your own room. No one would want to stay with you anyway." He strolled to the front. "My name's Ricky Jackson, and I'm Rock Star."

"In your dreams," Pretty Boy said behind his hand on a cough, but Ricky ignored him.

"My favorite kind of music is rock, but I can pretty much play any instrument in any style. Since I was alone in the band room when the meteorite hit my school, I can now play them all at the same time." He stood there looking human one minute and like an octopus the next. His arms and legs multiplied and transformed until he resembled a full orchestra, and then he began to play the most beautiful music in perfect pitch.

Pretty Boy yawned, strode to the front of the room as though he were a king, and faced us with a smug look. "Step aside, Rock Loser, and let someone who has real talent take the floor."

# 6

# LAB

Ricky the Rock Star's eyes reduced to slits. For a moment, I thought he would stand up to the pretty boy, but then he backed down and took his seat.

The boy before us was super-hot, with strawberry blond hair, perfect features, and a killer body--but he acted so cocky that his attitude actually made him unattractive. "Name's Kyle Kensington, but you may refer to me as King Cable."

"Oh, my God, you're a couch potato?" Amy gaped at him, as shocked as we all were. "I've never met any couch potato who looks like that."

"I like TV. They have a fitness channel. Duh. Shows how little you know." He snorted, really looking ugly now. Amy scowled and looked like she wanted to say something, but Kyle cut her off. "Anyway, I was watching my favorite show in my bedroom when the meteorite came crashing through my window. Now I come with a permanent flat screen built right in." He held his hand out before us, and his palm became a universal remote control.

"The best part is I'm the star of a never-ending episode called life. That's right, peasants. I can control any room I'm in, so I'd think twice before ticking me off."

Amy scoffed. "You're such a--" She froze like a wax statue, her mouth hanging open.

"Careful, Athletic Cup, or you'll cough up a Ping-Pong ball," King Cable said, his thumb firmly holding down the pause button.

"Knock it off," Ricky said, "or I'll--or I'll--or I'll--"

"Mr. Kensington, that is quite enough," Dr. Guggenheim said sternly.

"Fine." Kyle took Ricky off repeat and Amy off pause. "Sorry, sir, it won't happen again," he said as he sat down, but he didn't look sorry at all.

What was the government thinking, making this kid a superhero? And why was it every school always had to have a bully? I thought about my powers and everything I was capable of. Maybe it was time someone put him in his place, but I wasn't exactly sure how.

"Okay, class, buckle up for some excitement," Dr. Guggenheim announced. "It's time for lab."

---

OKAY, SO THIS LAB WASN'T LIKE ANY LAB I'D EVER BEEN IN. There were no lab tables, desks or chairs. In fact there wasn't anything except the eleven of us standing in our unitards, in a big, empty room with padded walls.

It reminded me of a nuthouse I'd once seen in a movie. Meanwhile, our professors sat safely behind a shatterproof glass wall at a long table with microphones, wearing head-phones as though they were announcers at some event.

So what did that make us--the main attraction?

Dr. Guggenheim tapped the microphone, clearing his throat and asking, "Can you hear me now?"

We nodded and then stood there like member of a rare species at a zoo while our spectators carefully watched and waited for us to do something. And like zoo animals, we obviously didn't understand their language.

Professor Troubadour leaned forward and spoke into her microphone. "Boys and girls, don't be nervous. Just do what comes naturally to you. I will be observing how your actions affect your bodies." She picked up her pen in a ready position, appearing focused and serious, but her eyes sparkled even from this distance.

Professor Hillcrest nodded like a bobblehead mounted on a bumper car. He spoke into his microphone, his calm words and tone not matching the enthusiasm that rolled off him in waves. "That's right. This is no big deal, really. Just forget we're here, and let us observe what chemical reactions you undergo--or even cause, for that matter." His head bobbed faster, his eyes wide and his smile nearly blinding now.

Finally, Professor Westcott smiled kindly, her eyes sending encouragement as she joined in the conversation. "Look, I know you must feel like you're on display. Yes, you're the most exciting discovery we've made in decades. However, we're not the enemy. We're here to help. This is your chance to demonstrate exactly what you can do. Just like you did in the classroom--only here you're in a safe environment."

"Awesome, dudes, then you won't mind if I do this..." Warren aka Wheels transformed both legs into BMX bike tires. He peeled out across the floor, raced up the wall and started circling the room, gaining speed as he went. When he was traveling faster than information through cyberspace and literally burning rubber onto the wall, he switched his feet into inline skates and launched himself into the air.

He triple-flipped with a twist and landed on his hands, which he'd fused into a skateboard along the way. When we were so dizzy our heads were spinning, he righted himself, flicked Michaela's long, dark silky hair, and tossed her a grin as he sailed by.

Michaela, better known as Mechanica, reacted nearly as quickly as he had, transforming her arms into massive hedge clippers and chopping off two inches of his purple-streaked hair on just one side. He gasped when she barely missed his ear.

"Mess with my hair, pay the consequences." She smirked. "*Dude!*"

Warren whipped a hand up to his head, looking stunned for a moment, but then he turned to Francesca. "Hey, Fashionista, got a mirror?"

She shrugged. "Sure." Turning her palm into a mirror, she held her hand up before him.

He grabbed her wrist and looked closely at his reflection. A smile spread across his face and he beamed as he turned to Michaela. "Righteous!"

She ground her teeth and grunted. "Of course you'd think that you bucket of bolts."

Warren just laughed.

Francesca yanked her hand away. "Wash much?" She tipped her head to one side and soapy water poured out her ear. She scrubbed her hands clean of the wheel grease from his and then tipped her head to the other side and dried them with her blow-dryer ear. "Boys are such dirty little pigs."

"Who you calling dirty? Your friend Gunner Girl over there is dirtier than any boy I've ever met," Ricky said, jerking his head to the side toward Gi, his Afro bouncing once.

"I had no beef with you until now, Rock Star." Gi shook her arm, and it changed into a fully loaded paintball machine gun. She aimed it at Ricky's head and said, "You won't be such a shining star by the time I get done with you."

Ricky's eyes grew enormous, and he clapped his hands into two huge cymbals, holding them up seconds before puke-green paintballs splattered what would have been his face. He let out a loud wail that sounded like a tuba and flushed crimson. "Ex-*cuse* me?"

Gi scoffed. "There's no excuse for you."

Hope flew into action, spitting dandelion-yellow lethal cleaning solution all over the floor in true Home Ec Helper fashion. She changed her feet into Swiffer mops and glided across the linoleum like an ice dancer competing in the Olympics, even throwing in a sit spin.

"Don't clean up his mess," Gi said. "Forget fighting with each other. It's girls against boys from now on. He called me dirty."

"Well, you sort of are." Hope bit her bottom lip, looking undecided as she glanced at Parker, the Picasso Kid.

Parker smiled with adoration at Hope, and a bright-red heart tattoo blossomed just above the neckline of his unitard.

Gi's eyes traveled back and forth between the two of them, and then she threw her hands up. "I might be messy, but I'm not dirty. There's a big difference. Some roomy you are. You can't side with them. What happened to loyalty?"

"Sorry," Hope said, looking chagrinned. "I didn't know we were at war. Why can't we all just get along?"

Kyle rolled his eyes. "Look, Martha Junior, this isn't a TV show. You skirts stay away from us guys, and we'll all get along just fine."

"Who are you calling a skirt, and who even uses that word anyway, you lazy bench-sitter? You're just jealous because someone is prettier than you are." Amy marched over to Kyle and started yelling in his face. "Why I bet you're the one who wears a--"

Her lips still moved a mile a minute, but no sound came out. She grabbed her throat and looked horrified, like she might stay on mute forever. Her face turned red, and actual steam hissed out her ears as her hands picked up the pace triple time.

At last, Amy looked like she'd had enough. She tightened her impressive abs, and her stomach changed to Jell-O once more. She reached in, pulled out a tennis ball, and transformed her arm into a racket. Tossing the ball high in the air, she wound up to serve the sucker straight at Kyle's smug smile.

Kyle simply punched a key on his remote-control hand and kept replaying the entire scene from the second he'd put her on mute to just before her serve. Over and over and over until she looked exhausted and furious at the same time.

Brent fused his hands together, becoming Boy-X. His eyes grew focused and intense as he rapidly played a video game. He'd obviously won, if the triumphant expression on his face was any indication. Then he pressed a button, and an enormous monster--fangs, claws, and all--magically appeared out of thin air directly in front of Kyle.

For a minute, Kyle backed up in surprise, genuine fear

flashing across his gorgeous face. Recovering quickly, he pressed the rewind button before the monster could shred him to bits. After hitting 'Play,' he waited until the part where Brent had started to fuse his hands together, and then Kyle hit pause.

Everyone stared at Kyle as though he really was a King and they had no idea how to stop his tyrannical rule. The power had gone straight to his head. He started to hit another button, when, as if in slow motion--but in reality, faster than the speed of light--my GPS brain anticipated his next move.

My auto-response function to counter danger kicked into gear. Squeezing my eyes shut, I pressed my temples. The motor neurons in my cerebrum carried an electronic pulse down my spine and straight to my cell palm. My hand tingled as I flung it in the King's direction, blocking the signal to his cable palm and knocking him off his throne. Just like that, the room came to life once more as everyone was taken off hold.

With a yelp, Kyle stumbled back a few steps. He shook his hand which was now smoking. My own fingertips were glowing bright green. At one time, that alone would have sent me in a panic, but not here, not now. I was no longer alone, I realized, and a calm feeling settled over me like a screen protector.

A high-pitched screeching noise sounded, like the kind you hear from the Emergency Alert System when they conduct their occasional tests on everyone's TV's. Only I'd intercepted and personalized the message for Kyle's channel, and the sound echoed out his ears in a robotic voice.

WE INTERRUPT THIS BROADCAST TO ISSUE A WARNING FROM YOUR

*Emergency Butt-kicking Superhero Leader. This is not a Test. I repeat, this is not a test. A cease-and-desist warning has been issued. Failing to heed this warning will put you in imminent danger. Now back to your regularly scheduled program.*

KYLE BLINKED A COUPLE TIMES, AS THOUGH COMING BACK TO reality, and stared at me in wonder and a little fear. He looked like he was thinking about his next move when a loud crash came from the teacher observation room.

We all whipped around to stare through the window. At first I thought maybe one of the professors had had a heart attack over our out-of-control display. But then Dr. Guggenheim spoke through the microphone, looking upset as he adjusted his thick glasses.

"There's been an accident, boys and girls. Class dismissed."

---

LATER THAT NIGHT, WE WERE ALL SHAKEN AS WE GATHERED IN our common room. Soon after, the boys' RA, Lance Anderson, joined us. He wore a pale-yellow golf shirt with chinos and loafers, and he had jet-black hair neatly combed forward and gentle blue eyes. On anyone else, the look would have been nerdy, but it made him look like a knight in shining armor. I liked him immediately. It figured that the boys would get a gentle hero while we were stuck with the devil warden.

Sir Lancelot paced in front of us looking troubled. He rubbed his hands together and then finally stopped and faced us. "First, let me say Professor Troubadour is going to be all right. She's resting comfortably in the hospital, but unfortunately, she won't be back with us."

"What exactly happened to her anyway?" I asked.

"The lighting fixture came loose and fell on top of her. It's a good thing she leaned forward to speak into her microphone just seconds before. Had she been sitting upright at the time, the fixture probably would have killed her."

We sucked in air and looked at each other in alarm.

"Some safety room." Brent shook his head. "Kind of ironic that she got hurt in there, don't you think?"

"Not ironic," Agent Maxwell said, stepping into the room.

I hadn't seen him since he'd brought me here. Having him show up now gave me a funny feeling in my gut. I'd come to learn my gut was usually right.

"If it's not ironic, then what is it?" I asked.

"Deliberate." Agent Maxwell pulled off his sunglasses and looked me square in the eye. "That lighting fixture didn't fall by itself. Someone cut the cables. An amateur by the looks of it."

"What does that mean?" Sir Lancelot asked.

"That means we have a mole."

We all started talking at once, and Lance held up his hands. "I know this is disturbing, guys. But relax. Tracy and I are both here for you." Warden Robbins joined his side and nodded. "We won't let anything happen to you, okay?" I knew there was no "we" when it came to protecting *me*, but I believed in him. "Let's remain calm and quiet so we can hear what else Agent Maxwell has to say."

Dark Shades Man nodded once at Sir Lancelot, and then continued. "Someone is trying to sabotage this program by taking out your professors--and possibly even you. Rest assured we're looking into the matter. In the meantime, I suggest you stop fighting each other and start acting like a team. Get some sleep. You're going to need it."

He left, and so did our RA's. For a minute, we all just stared at each other. Somehow, no words were necessary for each of us to understand...A truce had been formed.

# 7

# TRUCE

week later, we all sat in a large room filled with small tables. Our families sat across from us like a scene right out of a prison movie.

Visiting day.

So far, no more incidents had happened. Maybe we weren't in any real danger after all. Maybe it had been a test to see if we could work as a team. I mean, they let our families come visit today, so things couldn't be that bad.

"How's my girl, Sammy? They treating you okay?" Gram asked, giving our FBI "guards"--stationed around the four corners of the room to watch us closely--the evil eye.

"It's okay. I'm learning a lot." I sent her a meaningful look that said, *I can't fill you in now, but I'll find a way. There are eyes and ears everywhere in here.* "Where are Mom and Dad?" I knew Dad was in LA with Simon, but I still held out hope he would find a way to show up.

"Well, your dad couldn't make it because his intern program had a crisis that left him short-handed." She paused for a moment. "Simon left."

"What?" I was stunned. "That's all Simon talked about for weeks. What happened to make him leave?"

"His favorite uncle's gone missing, and his parents pulled him out. Now your dad has to find a replacement."

"Wait a minute." I shook my head, trying to understand what she was telling me. "The uncle who Simon is named after, and who spoke at the seminar last fall?"

"One and the same." Gram shrugged. "I guess he didn't get some grant he'd been counting on, and he was really upset. Now no one can find him."

"Poor Simon. He must be worried sick and so bummed because he had to leave the program early and come back to Blue Lake."

"I heard his spirits were pretty low, but your little friend Maria is tickled pink to have him home again. Don't you worry. She'll look after that boy. People say she hasn't let him out of her sight since he got back."

I grinned. That sounded just like Maria. Then my smile slipped as loneliness crept in. "What about Mom?"

Gram rolled her eyes and let out a grunt. "That woman's crazy. She came all the way here ready to scale the walls and bust you out when you didn't check in on that new cell phone she bought you. Took everything I had to rein her in and convince her you were okay, and that the school didn't allow calls to home for the first couple of weeks. She doesn't like this setup any more than I do, but I knew you needed time to...you know, figure things out." She winked. "I had to get your dad to pull some strings and call in a few favors at Electro so they would swamp her at work and keep her busy. Trust me; you don't want her here in her frame of mind right now."

"Thanks, Gram." I felt better knowing that my parents at least wanted to see me and kind of relieved that Gram had stepped in. Something fishy was going on around here. But even if I could find a way to escape, the Girl Scout in me was guilting me into sticking around and doing the right thing.

"So, *have* you figured things out?" Gram asked quietly.

My eyes scanned the room, and I lowered my voice. "Some. It's complicated."

"That's what I thought." Gram sighed. "Nothing's ever easy. Well, you take all the time you want, but let me know if you need anything." She leaned forward. "Anything at all. I don't care who's listening." She nodded once, then reached across the table and hugged me hard.

"Thanks, Gram. You know I will."

She stood. "See you in two weeks, rain or shine. Just let 'em try and stop me. I'll bring your mother here myself, and then they'll wish they'd never met any of us." She stuck her nose in the air and marched out of the room.

---

LATER THAT EVENING, EVERYONE HAD GONE BACK TO THEIR rooms since our curfew bell was due to ring soon. I was feeling really down. Everyone's families had come to visit them, but all I'd gotten to see was Gram.

I adored Gram, and I understood why my parents couldn't come, but I really missed Mom and Dad. And Mel! I was going crazy not getting to talk to her, but if I tried to use my cell hand, "they" would intercept my call and I'd be in huge trouble. Mel probably thought I'd totally ditched her.

"Hey Fabulastic Sam," Brent said as he wandered into the mini-kitchen for a bottle of water. He'd just gotten done working out, and his body was damp and a little shiny. He wore running shorts and a tank top that showed off his well-toned muscles. He might not be as muscular as Trevor, but he was in great shape, and those killer dimples were going to get me into serious trouble yet.

Even so, I sighed long and hard in response, unable to enjoy the vision in front of me. I couldn't help it. He'd interrupted me smack dab in the middle of a major pity party.

"Let me guess...not feeling so fabulastic?" He plopped down on the couch next to me and took a long swig from the bottle of water he'd just uncapped.

"Not so much," I said.

"Why?" He lifted a shoulder. "You just got to see your family today. I would think you'd be feeling great."

"No, *you* got to see your family. I got to see my Gram. My parents couldn't make it, but my best friend is the one I'm really missing. I'm used to talking to her every day, and I promised I would text her."

He hesitated for a minute and then finally said, "Is that all you're worried about? So text her."

"I can't." I leaned in close and whispered, "Big Brother has eyes and ears everywhere."

"Not everywhere." A mischievous smile played at the corners of his lips. "I know a way," he said quietly.

My pulse kicked in to hyperdrive. "What are you talking about?"

He looked around and then locked eyes with me, his dimples sinking deep. "Come on." He grabbed my arm and pulled me to my feet.

"Where are we going?" I asked, jogging after him.

"To the workout room."

"We have a workout room?" I vaguely remembered Special Agent Crawford mentioning a gym when we first arrived, but working out wasn't a high priority for me these days.

"Just a small one off to the side by the elevator."

"Oh, that room. I thought that was just the janitor and maintenance man's supply closet."

"That's in the back of the gym."

"But, I don't want to work out," I whined.

"Sure you do. It will clear your head," he said in a voice much louder than necessary.

"Whatever." At this point I was too tired to argue.

He pulled me into a small gym and headed for the closet in the back corner, outside the range of the cameras. Scanning the room one last time, he yanked open the closet, shoved me inside, and then hopped in beside me and shut the door.

"What are you doing?" I squeaked.

"Shhhh." He pressed a finger against my lips, and I couldn't talk if my life depended on it.

The pressure cooker within me bubbled furiously, but no 911 calls were blocked. It was kind of nice to be able to feel something, anything, and not be afraid of what would happen.

Like a normal teenager for a change.

Brent took a moment to make sure the coast was clear and then snapped me out of my daydream with his words. "We're safe for now, but we've got to move fast."

"Okay, then." I tossed my hands up in defeat. "I guess I could do a little Zumba, but this closet isn't exactly big enough." I started to shake my hips, swing my arms, and hum a crazy beat like I'd seen my mom do with her personal trainer.

Brent grabbed my hips to still their movement. "Shhh, someone's going to hear you." He grinned at me funny and shook his head. "Dancing isn't what I had in mind."

My internal circuits sparked as my pulse picked up

speed. Exactly what *did* he have in mind, and what was going to happen if Francesca found out? Not wanting to risk it, I placed my hand on the knob ready to go. In an instant, he stopped me.

"Brent, what's going on?"

He shrugged, and even in the dim light, I could see his cheeks go pink. "Nothing. You just looked so down. I'm trying to grant your wish. But hey, if dancing makes you feel better, then knock yourself out. You kind of looked like you were about to anyway." He did laugh this time.

I smacked him on the arm. "Funny." Then couldn't help laughing along with him. "Okay, Mr. Wish Granter, what are you, a genie or something?"

"Or something." His grin was back, and so was Mr. Adorable.

"Well, then, I'm all yours," I responded. Then I realized how it sounded and felt my ears burn off like the time I fried my hard drive.

His grin widened. "Now you're talking."

OMG! Francesca would kill me if I gave him the wrong impression. "I meant--"

"Never mind that, just sit still for a minute." He fused his hands together and started playing a video game.

"Are you kidding me? Now is not the time to play some game."

He shushed me. "Now is the perfect time to play a game, and I need to win, so be quiet please."

I gave up on trying to figure boys out. "Whatever."

Five minutes later, after a few grumbles mixed with a couple whoops, he finally hissed, "*Yes!* I did it."

"Did what?" I was almost afraid to ask.

"Won the EMP function."

"The what?"

"The electro magnetic pulse function."

"English, please. What does that mean?"

"That means for a short period of time, I can turn off any electronics in the room. Since we're in the closet, that includes the bigger room the closet is part of. I just didn't want anyone to figure out what I was doing before I could turn everything off." He put his hands on my shoulders, and I almost forgot to breathe. "Sam, it means you can call your friend Mel without them blocking the transmission or listening in."

I almost cried. "*You* are the one who's fabulous, Brent. I don't know how I'm going to thank you."

"You can thank me later," he said, his eyes twinkling, and then he pressed a few buttons and the lights flickered. "Okay, the cameras, listening devices, and intercepting systems are off, but hurry up. I don't know how long it will last."

I whipped off my glove and dialed Mel as fast as I could.

"Where have you been?" Mel shrieked. "You were supposed to text me every day, but you haven't sent a word."

"I know. Long story. Call Gram for details," I blurted. "We don't have much time, so tell me everything."

"Scott broke up with me," she wailed.

I sucked in a breath, shock messages whizzing from my ears to my brain via my sensory neurons and then shooting down my spine on the backs of my motor neurons until every cell in my body vibrated with rage.

"Are you kidding me?" My heart jumped in my throat, and I wished I could hug her. "Why would he do that?"

"I don't know, maybe because he's an idiot. When Trevor was dating you and I was your best friend, everything was wonderful. But now that you're gone and Trevor asked one of the Petterelli twins to the dance, Scott dumped me so he could ask the other one."

"Then he doesn't deserve you." Anger surged through me on a wave of heat, and my skin glowed pink. The next time I saw Scott, I planned to tell him exactly what I thought of him. Then Mel's words sank in, and I felt the blood leave my face like the juice out of a laptop battery. "Wait a minute," I swallowed hard, "Trevor asked someone else to the dance?" The breath whooshed out of me.

Brent arched a brow and frowned. I gave him a weak smile and hoisted a shoulder, acting like Trevor was nobody.

"Yeah. *Now* do you see why I needed you?" Mel's voice hitched. "Everything is a mess!"

"No kidding," I responded on barely more than a whisper. I couldn't even tell her about Brent because (a) he was standing right here, and (b) she just got dumped, and (c) Trevor was moving on! I knew it was what I wanted, what needed to happen, but I couldn't deny a small part of my heart had withered up and died after hearing that news.

"When are you coming home?" she asked, sounding miserable.

"I don't know, and I'm so sorry. It's insane here, too. I mean it, call Gram. She'll explain everything."

"This is stupid."

"I know. Love you, Mels. I *will* find a way to talk to you again soon, I promise, but I've got to go now before I get caught."

"Fine, whatever." She sniffed. "But there's one more thing you should know."

What else could possibly have happened, I wondered. "Okay, what?"

"Your mom is dating Trevor's dad, Sheriff Hamilton."

"*Whaaat*?" I shrieked, and just like that the EMP function quit and my cell hand disconnected.

"Who's Trevor, and what was that all about?" Brent asked, his face looking suspicious and not too happy.

I was struggling for an answer when the closet door burst open and Special Agent Crawford stood before us looking royally peeved.

The curfew bell went off.

Her eyes narrowed as they traveled back and forth between us. "Someone better start talking fast," was all she said.

I heard shuffling and footsteps behind her and peeked around to the side to see. Everyone had scrambled out of their rooms and followed Special Agent Crawford to see what was going on.

"Um, I, well...it was an accident." I stumbled over the broom as I tried to step out of the closet.

Brent caught me, held me a couple seconds too long, and then stared into my eyes. "It was no accident."

"I-It wasn't?" I asked, helpless to do anything but gaze back at him. Everything got deathly silent.

"I did it," he said. "I've wanted to kiss Sam since I first saw her." Gasps rang out around us, mine the loudest.

"Y-You did?" I gulped.

He winked, clueing me in that this was all just a made up story to use as a cover-up of what we'd really been doing--talking to someone on the "outside." If anyone found out, we'd be in real trouble for sure. I had to give Brent an A for effort. He was one heck of an actor.

He'd had me fooled!

He faced Special agent Crawford. "After our introductions in class and lab the other day, I knew that if I just kissed her, she'd block a 911 call or set off all the alarms or something."

"So you improvised," Special Agent Crawford studied him, her head tilted slightly to the side, deciding whether or not to believe him.

"Exactly." He looked down at his sneaker, which was scuffing the carpet. "Except I was only trying to shut *Sam* off, not whatever else I must have scrambled. Sorry. It won't happen again."

After a full tense moment, she finally nodded. "I hope it was worth it, Matthews, because you've earned detention for you both. Dating a member of your team is not advised for any of you. It could compromise a mission someday. Now I suggest you get to bed." She spun on her heel. "That goes for the rest of you."

Everyone hurried back to their rooms, Francesca lagging behind. She shot me a loof full of hurt and betrayal, and then she was gone. She had no clue the whole story was a cover-up and that I hadn't betrayed her at all, no matter how much I might have wanted to at the time.

I turned to Brent. "Thanks for helping me talk to Mel, and double thanks for covering for me. I just wish you didn't have to get in trouble because of a lie."

"Who said it was a lie?" He flicked my cheek with his finger and then jogged off, leaving me totally shell-shocked.

Brent Matthews wanted to kiss me, too? Oh, boy, we were in big trouble now, especially now that I knew he could. EMP was a beautiful thing. I exhaled dreamily. Special Agent Crawford was right. Dating was so not a good idea, because now that I knew Brent liked me, I'd be thinking about little else.

Except maybe brooms and closets and kisses--oh my!

# 8

## POP QUIZ

"Did Brent kiss you or didn't he? That's all I want to know?" Francesca said, rubbing her temples like she had a headache. Her eyes changed from amber to a bright jealous green.

It was late and all I wanted to do was go to sleep, but my suite-mates wouldn't let me. We might be confined to our rooms since it was past curfew, but they weren't going to sleep until I caved and gave them the scoop.

"No." I sat on Francesca's bed beside her and whispered, "I told you he was just covering for me so I could call my best friend Mel. You know, the one on the outside." I made a set of air quotes, thinking at least I'd told the truth.

"So you don't like each other then?" She eyed me suspiciously.

I shook my head, my ponytail swinging in front of my shoulder. Okay, not the whole truth. I quickly amended, "I mean, I think he's cute and all, but you called first dibs. I plan to honor that."

Besides, the more I thought about it, the more I suspected Brent had just been teasing me. He did that a lot.

And with all that was going on, we really didn't need the complication of "liking" each other or kissing or whatever.

Francesca relaxed. "You're a good friend."

"I'm trying to be." I laughed. "It's not always easy."

"I know, right? He's so dreamy. I just wish he would pay attention to me." She looked confused. "I'm not used to guys who don't pay attention to me. Brent just looks at me like he looks at everyone else. I mean, what's it going to take for him to pull *me* into a broom closet?"

"A cell phone in your hand." I giggled, and she whacked me with a pillow on a giggle of her own.

Hope walked into our room, handing us a huge bowl of popcorn, passing out napkins, and wiping her fingers on her apron. She sat down on the other bed beside Gi. "I'd give anything for Parker to pull me into a broom closet and kiss me, but you heard what Special Agent Crawford said. Dating a team member is not advised.

"Looks like the only kisses I'll be getting from Parker will probably be in chocolate form--or a tattoo. I think it's so adorable when he does that." She pouted. "Oh well, my poisonous breath is lethal anyway. If he kissed me, the toxic cleaning fluids on my tongue would probably kill him. This stinks."

"If you ask me, kissing any one of those boys would stink. Especially Ricky the Rock-headed Rockstar." Gi shot caramel-flavored edible paintballs all over her popcorn and dug in.

Amy and Michaela walked in, carrying sodas for us all, and then sat on the floor between the beds.

"I hear that, sister," Michaela added. "If Warren the streaky-headed freak whizzes by me patting any part of my body just one more time, I'll cut off more than a hunk of his hair. That boy is in serious need of a chill pill."

"Ha! Try being me. If Kyle puts me on pause or mute ever again, I'm going to permanently scramble his pretty face. We'll see what kind of reception he gets after that." Amy's stomach rumbled, but she wasn't hungry. The bowling balls were rolling around in her bottomless pit again. They tended to do that when she got worked up.

"Forget fighting with the boys," I said. "Remember our truce?"

Everyone grumbled.

"I still can't figure out if we're in danger or not. I mean, nothing else has happened. If it's just a test, then we need to go back to planning our escape. Trust me, the last thing you want is to be tied down working for the government. My parents do, and they have no life," I said.

"I thought you had to be seventeen to be recruited or drafted into the Special Forces," Francesca said.

"Guess we're the exception," Gi answered.

"I have plans," Amy added. "College scholarships to win and a pro soccer team to play for. I don't have time for any Phenoteen missions."

"I've never been big on being part of a team," Michaela said. "Got my own plans. A garage to open and some classic cars to restore. I say let the government do their own dirty work."

"Easier said than done," added Hope. "Don't get me wrong. I'd love to be the next Martha Stewart, but I don't see that happening unless we find a way to escape."

"Exactly." I looked them each in the eye. "They want us to work as a team? We'll give them a team. And our first mission will be Operation Freedom."

OUR RA'S, TRACY ROBBINS AND LANCE ANDERSON, STOOD IN the common room, checking off our names on a chart. "All present and accounted for," Sir Lancelot said on a smile.

"Oh, joy," Warden Robbins responded on a scowl, her spiked hair extra gelled today, making her look even scarier.

"Why'd you sign up for this anyway?" Lance asked, shaking his dark head.

"So I could get into the intern program. Duh. You can't tell me you like baby-sitting."

"I don't mind," he answered. "Besides, they're not babies. They're superheroes." He beamed at us, and Tracy just rolled her eyes. "Everyone ready to go?"

We all nodded and headed to the elevator. Just before we reached the doors, Frank Brown, the maintenance man, and Chuck Smith, the janitor, came out of the gym.

"Tell Special Agent Crawford everything's all set in there. All systems go and fully operational," Chuck said.

"Oh, and the bus is all set out front," Frank added. "Have fun today, but be careful. It's a jungle out there." He saluted us, and then they both took the stairs.

"Will do," Lance hollered after them just as the elevator doors opened and Professor Hillcrest stood waiting for us.

Since everything had been quiet for a week, he was taking our chemistry class on a field trip out into the real world to see how we worked as a team.

The bus ride to downtown Washington, DC, was a bit awkward. We'd all agreed to call a truce, but that still didn't mean we really liked each other.

Speaking of liking, I made sure I sat on the inside of the seat, closest to the window, while Francesca sat right by the aisle. Brent got on right after we did and sat in the row directly across from ours. He tried to start a conversation with me a couple times, but I just gave him one--or two--

word responses and kept staring out the window until he gave up.

Francesca leaned over and whispered in my ear. "I never said you couldn't talk to him, Sam. You're making things weird."

"Sorry," I whispered back, "but things *are* weird after the broom closet episode."

Neither one of us spoke for the rest of the ride. We weren't the only ones feeling the awkwardness. Warren kept tweaking Michaela's tools. Gi kept threatening to fine-tune Ricky's instrument. Parker kept blossoming with more tattoos every time Hope made goo-goo eyes at him. And Kyle was being a pain in everyone's butt, especially Amy's, with his annoying remote control hand.

Thankfully, the bus reached our destination before anyone really became out of control. Professor Hillcrest stood up and faced us. "The reason I brought you on this field trip is because I want you all to realize how important this program is. You should feel honored to be a part of something so groundbreaking that could affect the way we protect and defend our nation.

"We live in the greatest country in the world. It's not always easy to keep her safe." He looked us each in the eye. "But she's worth it. Since Washington, DC, is the heart of our country, I thought it was time you got to know her and see what you're fighting for."

We all filed off, tightening our coats against the chilly air and blowing snow as we joined our professor and our RA's at the curb in front of the National Archives Building. I felt like I was caught in the middle of a *National Treasure* movie as we went inside and looked at The Declaration of Independence, The Bill of Rights, and The Constitution on display.

Next we went on a tour and saw the Washington Monument, the Kennedy Center, the White House, the U.S. Supreme Court, and even the U.S. Capital. Finally, we ended up at the Smithsonian Institute. We didn't have time to tour the National Zoo, but we did get to see the Air and Space Museum and the American History Museum. The Natural History Museum was my favorite, except I kept waiting for the dinosaur in the front lobby to come to life and roar at me like in the movies.

While walking back to our rendezvous spot with our bus, Professor Hillcrest said, "I know you all live in different states, but that doesn't make them any less important to protect. That doesn't mean you're alone. You guys are lucky. You have each other. You must learn to set aside your differences and work together as a team. We'll focus more on that in Lab when we get back to the campus."

The professor led the way with everyone in between and Francesca and me bringing up the rear.

"Pssst," Francesca whispered in my ear again.

"What?" I whispered back.

"I think I just found my broom closet." She giggled.

"What the heck does that mean?" I blinked at her.

"You'll see." She jogged ahead, snagged Brent's hand, and then pulled him into a dark alley off to the side.

Oh, my gosh, what was I supposed to do? She was crazy, and we were for sure going to get in big trouble. I was getting ready to go in after her when someone let out a scream.

The rest of the Phenoteens joined me, with Professor Hillcrest and our RA's bringing up the rear, breathing hard and looking alarmed. We ran into the alley way, blinking to adjust our eyes to the dim light.

A big, burly bald man in a black-leather jacket with

enormous biceps and lots of tattoos had his arm wrapped around Francesca's neck and a massive knife pointing toward her jugular. Brent took a step back, looking dumbfounded.

Francesca's ear wasn't facing Baldy so she couldn't blast him away or scald him with hot water. All she could do was change her appearance which would only be useful if she'd already escaped and needed a disguise. But that didn't stop her nervous system from short-circuiting and causing her colors to change like a disco ball spinning out of control.

"I'm sorry, guys. I don't know what happened." Brent looked embarrassed and ashamed. "Francesca pulled me in here, and the guy grabbed her in like two seconds."

"Clam up, kid, or the pretty babe gets it," the monster of a man spoke in a super-deep voice.

"Relax, sir." Professor Hillcrest held up his hands and spoke in a calm voice, even though the vein in his neck was pulsing rapidly. "Tell us what you want and nobody has to get hurt."

Sir Lancelot didn't look like a knight in shining armor right now as he stood by the professor with his knees shaking. And Warden Robbins so did not look tough with her jaw hitting the floor and eyes bugging wide.

"Give me all of your money--and the kids', too," Baldy demanded. "Empty your pockets, throw the money at my feet, and then back off."

"D-Don't do what he says, guys." Francesca squeaked bravely while looking terrified. "You can take him. Remember who we are."

"Shut up," the guy snapped, tightening his grip. "You're nothing, none of you. Now do as I said."

Only, we *were* something.

We were Phenoteens, and we all seemed to realize that

at once. Embracing our inner superheroes, everyone reached in their pockets slowly--and then things got crazy. Everyone was trying to be the hero, and no one was working together. Being the only one with past experience, I knew exactly how fast things could go wrong.

My computer brain kicked into high gear, allowing me to assess the situation in a microburst of speed. The information was processed in my cerebellum, and the outcome was anticipated. Oh boy, not good. I reached forward and hit the slow-motion button on King Cable's hand, and gave each member of my team instructions on what I wanted them to do.

Kyle might be able to control the room we were in, but we quickly found the effect only lasted for a matter of minutes. The scene before me resumed at full speed, and I could only hope my fellow teammates were up to the task.

Gunner Girl cocked and loaded her handgun, firing off several rounds of black paintballs in Baldy's face. Momentarily blinded, he still didn't loosen his hold on Fashionista. Rock Star didn't waste any time in racing forward, transforming his hands into cymbals along the way. When he reached the bad guy, he wound up and clapped them hard over both of Baldy's ears. Baldy let out a howl but still didn't let go of his death grip on Francesca--or the deadly knife in his hand.

Wheels transformed his feet into rollerblades, let out a sharp whistle, and raced to Mechanica's side. As he zoomed by, he scooped her into his arms. For once, she didn't complain. She shrugged as though she realized if you can't beat 'em, join 'em--and she did exactly that. She let him carry her as he picked up speed, using Baldy's temporary blindness and loss of hearing to his advantage. Mechanica transformed her hand into a metal saw along the way and cut off the blade of Baldy's knife.

Baldy's hand slipped and he loosened his hold on Fashionista. She spun around and used boiling water from her ear to scald the arm that had been wrapped around her neck. Baldy let out a yelp while Boy-X, who had been furiously playing a video game the whole time, won his match and made an electric scooter appear before him. He hopped on and raced to Francesca's side at full speed. She gladly stepped on, wrapping her arms tight around Brent's waist as if having her life threatened had been worth it for that one small act.

Seconds after they scootered out of the reach of Baldy, the robber looked furious and fully functional once more. King Cable quickly put the bad guy on pause while Athletica tumbled down the alley doing back handsprings. She ended with a high aerial of triple flips into a full layout, snagging a dangling rope from the side of the building on her way down to stick a perfect landing.

I didn't waste any time in googling the best Girl Scout knot I could. I'd never won a badge for knot tying in the past, but that was all about to change today. I hurried to tie a perfect knot even Houdini wouldn't have been able to escape from.

Meanwhile, the Picasso Kid painted a graffiti message for the cops on the canvas of his stomach and then used his internal light to burn the message on the wall of the building. As he finished up, Home Ec Helper stitched the rip in Fashionista's costume and scoured away our fingerprints.

"Great job, guys. Now let's get out of here before we have some major explaining to do to the cops." We weren't back in our prison cell, and my fear had set off several car alarms around the area. I led the way to the opening of the alley, fully intending to escape.

Just before we exited, Professor Hillcrest started clapping his hands. "And that, my friends, is why Digital Diva is your team leader." The car alarms still wailed, but no cop sirens could be heard.

We all skidded to a stop and gaped at the man.

"I have to say, Ray, you've got yourself an impressive group of soldiers here." Baldy stood up, free of the knot I'd painstakingly tied, and looked completely unharmed. Houdini might not be able to escape from my knot, but apparently, a highly trained individual could.

"Did I miss the memo? What's going on," I asked, plopping my hands on my hips. This had better not be what I thought it was. The bad feeling in my gut told me I wasn't going to like his answer to my question. "Is this a test?"

Professor Hillcrest just smiled widely and said, "More like a pop quiz, but no worries, you all passed with flying colors."

# 9

# DANGER 102

We were all on the bus headed back to the campus, royally fuming. The nerve of them to put us through a test like that! Someone could have been seriously hurt.

"Can you believe Baldy was special ops?" I asked Francesca.

"I know!" she shrieked. "That knife was no fake. It was very real--and sharp. I mean, that's just wrong. I don't care that he said he wouldn't have actually hurt me. Accidents happen."

"It was kind of cool how we handled ourselves, though," I admitted. I was still mad, but in a way, I was proud. We had rocked that alley.

"We couldn't have done it without you, Sam," Francesca said quietly. "You were amazing." She looked me in the eye. "You *are* amazing, and I am the one who hasn't been a very good friend. If you and Brent really do like each other, then you should go for it. He obviously doesn't like me. You should have seen his face when I dragged him into that alley."

"What happened?"

"I told him I was cold and needed warming up. That this was *our* broom closet, and to feel free to kiss me any time." Francesca didn't look embarrassed at all.

"Ohmigosh...what'd he do?" I asked, knowing I would never have had that kind of courage.

"Silly boy gave me a horrified look and started running out of the alley." She looked disgusted. "That's when Baldy grabbed me."

"I'm sure Brent was just surprised."

"Um, no. I'm smart enough to know when a guy isn't interested. I'm just not used to being on the receiving end." She shrugged, not really looking upset. "I'm chalking it up as a learning experience for how I treat the next guy I dump. Believe me, I'll be a little nicer about it. As for Brent, I'm way too cute to hang around a boy who's too blind to notice. He's all yours, chica."

"B-But, what if I don't want him?" I asked, suddenly terrified now that the thought of having him was a possibility.

She laughed. "Oh you want him, all right. You're just not sure you can have him. I know the feeling. I had to break up with my boyfriend back home, too. But remember, out here, we're all in the same boat. I say go for it. What can it hurt? Besides, you'll never know if it was meant to be unless you try."

I glanced across the aisle and locked eyes with Brent. My heart still belonged to Trevor, but I knew we didn't stand a chance. At least with Brent there was a shot. He smiled. I smiled. And without the use of my Electro-infused circuitry, an unspoken message had been sent.

Except that I had no clue what to do about it.

The bus pulled up to the campus, and we all filed off one

by one. The professor was last, as was the protocol for all field trips. He thanked the driver and was about to exit when a loud explosion sounded, followed by a flash of light.

A hidden car bomb on the bus had gone off.

Smoke billowed out from every window, but none of us moved very fast. We all looked at each other wearily, sighing and groaning. Once the smoke cleared, Sir Lancelot pried open the bus doors and he and Warden Robbins climbed inside. Seconds later Lance appeared, carrying an unconscious Professor Hillcrest in his arms. Lance set the professor on the concrete and shouted, "Someone get Dr. Guggenheim. The professor's been hurt."

Warden Robbins climbed down from the bus, carrying a coughing bus driver who otherwise seemed okay. "Something weird is going on around here," she said, eying each of us as though we were the culprits. "Payback?"

"Are you kidding me?" I shrieked. "Like we would have had time to plant a car bomb." I scowled and then paled. "Hey, wait a minute. You mean this isn't another test?"

"Pop quiz," someone corrected.

"Whatever," I snapped. "The point is that if this wasn't another test, we're in danger for real."

Brent's eyes met mine, and then he looked at everyone else. "Forget Operation Freedom. We need to find the mole, or the next victim might be one of us."

LATER THAT EVENING, WE ALL SAT IN THE COMMON ROOM awaiting word. No one said much. The thought of finding the mole remained in our shocked minds. Finally, Special Agent Crawford waltzed off the elevator and joined us.

"Professor Hillcrest is doing fine. He suffered a concussion and inhaled a lot of smoke, but he will be okay. However, like Professor Troubadour, he will not be returning to IPR. Professor Westcott and Dr. Guggenheim will be your only teachers until this program is complete. Naturally they are concerned, as are all of you, I'm sure. But rest assured the FBI is on full alert.

"We are taking this matter very seriously and have stepped up security. And as of this moment, all further field trips have been cancelled indefinitely. You're not to leave the compound. Your RA's will see to it. In the meantime, you all need to practice honing your skills while we focus on catching whoever this mole is."

She spun around and marched out in the same no-nonsense manner in which she had appeared. We turned to each other, no one saying a word for several minutes as we all tried to make sense of what had just happened.

"Well, I'm going to bed." Warden Robbins stood and then looked over her shoulder. "You heard Special Agent Crawford. Any of you boneheads try to leave, your butt is mine. Beats going on some lame field trip any day." She turned back around and disappeared into the girls' wing.

"Ignore her," Sir Lancelot said. "The FBI is just trying to make sure we all stay safe. In the meantime, I'd work on fine-tuning your abilities in case the security inside these walls is breached." He shuddered. "It's getting pretty freaky around here." He got up and headed to his room in the boys' suite.

We all just sat there for a minute, looking lost. Someone had to say something, do something. Only, they were all looking at me. I groaned and finally said, "We can't just sit back and do nothing."

"Agreed," Brent added. "But what are we supposed to do, Boss?"

"I don't know. Look for suspects I guess," I responded, not feeling very boss-like. "Who knows about this program?"

"The FBI," someone said.

"Our professors," someone else said.

"The lunch lady," another person added.

"The groundskeeper," yet another person said.

"Hey, wait a minute," I chimed in. "The maintenance man and janitor both knew about our field trip and had access to the bus this morning. Where were they in the morning before they came to fix the cameras and clean up the gym?"

"Good question. That sounds like as good a place as any to start," Brent said. "We need a plan."

"Good. Then let's all sleep on it and talk after tomorrow morning's Lab. Operation Freedom is out. It's time we focused on Operation Find The Mole!" I nodded once, and we all headed to bed.

---

"I KNOW YOU'RE ALL SCARED, BECAUSE I'M EVEN SCARED," DR. Guggenheim said through the microphone in our new Lab room. He pushed his thick glasses up his nose, and the line down the center of his forehead deepened. "I'm just so relieved you were all off that bus before the bomb exploded."

He shook his head. "This is crazy. This is supposed to be a safe environment, but I have to say I'm not very impressed with the security measures around this place. I mean, Professor Hillcrest could have..." he cleared his throat, "could have died."

Professor Westcott patted the doctor's arm, leaning

forward and taking over the mic when it was clear the doctor was too upset to continue. "Don't worry, Doctor. The hospital says Professor Hillcrest will make a full recovery, same with Professor Troubadour." She smiled reassuringly at all of us.

"The FBI is doing all they can to catch the person responsible. No one else knows the details of this project, so the guilty culprit has to be someone on the inside. With the heightened security around here, it's only a matter of time before the person is caught. In the meantime, we have work to do."

Dr. Guggenheim placed his hand on Professor Westcott's shoulder. "Thank you, Carolyn, I'm better now." He took the mic back and looked at us, renewed excitement shining in his eyes. "Professor Hillcrest filled me in before you got on the bus yesterday. He was very impressed with the way you all worked as a team. When I call your names, come stand together in the middle of the room."

We all eyed each other warily.

"Gi Wong and Ricky Jackson. Warren Thompson and Michaela Delgado. Francesca Ferrari and Brent Matthews. Kyle Kensington and Amy Newlander. Parker Schofield and Hope O'Reilly."

Everyone grumbled because he'd chosen the people who butted heads the most to stand by each other. And he hadn't chosen me at all. I couldn't help wonder what it all meant. I didn't have to wait long to find out.

"Samantha Granger you're alone because you're the team captain. As for the rest of you, meet your new partners."

Great. Once again I was the loner.

Everyone started complaining at once, but Dr. Guggenheim held up his hand. "Quiet," he said sternly. "The couples I have chosen to work together are very passionate about their feelings toward one another. Love and hate relationships aren't all that different from each other. Passion is passion, and right now, I need you all to be passionate about this program.

"The animosity or affection you have for each other will only make you work that much harder. You kids *will* become a team, even if I have to make you spend twenty-four hours a day together. Do I make myself clear?"

Everyone grudgingly nodded their assent.

"Okay, boys and girls, if there are no further objections, let's begin class," Professor Westcott said.

I raised my hand.

"Yes, Miss Granger?" she asked.

"I don't feel so good. Can I go to the nurse?" I crossed my arms over my stomach and moaned.

"Oh, my. Well...sure, I guess," she said then added, "Why don't you have Miss Robbins escort you there."

The nurse's station wasn't located in our "special" wing, so going there meant having access to the outside world. They didn't like that unless we had a guard with us. In my case, the warden who hated me.

"Thanks," I said weakly and then headed for the door and joined the evilly grinning Amazon, Warden Robbins.

"Follow me, Granger," she said and led the way to the elevators. Once we were inside and the doors closed, she added, "Try something. I dare you." She rubbed her hands together slowly. "I'm in the mood for a good scrap."

Thinking quickly, I moaned louder and took a step toward her. "I think I'm going to throw up."

Her face paled and she pressed her back against the wall. "Puke on me, and you're a dead girl for sure."

I eyed her, wondering where'd she'd been yesterday

morning before we'd gotten on the bus. She sure had a lot of animosity. The elevator doors opened and she bolted, walking quickly so that I had to jog to keep up with her. We made our way past the lobby and the cafeteria, finally entering the nurse's office in the back.

"I'll be outside. Let me know when you're done." She exited the room, far away from me.

The nurse examined me from head to toe and then frowned. "I don't see anything that's obvious, but we have had several cases of the stomach flu. Why don't you lie down on that cot for a while, and we'll see if you feel better."

"Okay, thanks." I walked over to an open cot and pulled back the curtain. Slipping inside, I closed the curtain and lay down.

So far, none of us had come up with a plan. All we knew was that both the janitor and the maintenance man had known about the program, had had access to the bus, and had shown up late to our floor this morning. I'd faked being sick so I could see what I could find out. The school might have eyes and ears and be able to intercept a call from my cell hand, but they would have no clue if I did a little surfing on the net. I googled IPR and managed to find and download the floor plans to the massive building. I didn't have any idea what to look for, but it was a start.

The distinct sounds of someone getting sick came from the curtained cot next to me. The nurse moved the boy to another cot and called the janitor. Mr. Smith arrived within minutes, making quick work of cleaning up the mess.

Just before he left, the walkie-talkie strapped to his hip went off. I sat up quick and peeked out of the curtain.

"Chuck, you read me?" said the dispatcher's voice.

The janitor answered, "Read you loud and clear, Mary. What's up?"

"Frank Brown needs your help in Sector 4. The oil tank cracked while he was fixing the bus. There's oil everywhere."

"On my way," Chuck said and signed off with, "Over and out."

As soon as he left, I was on my way too. Because if the janitor and the maintenance man were both busy working in the garage in Sector 4, then their offices were free and clear. It was time for the Phenoteens to do a little work of their own.

# 10

## PHENO-SLEUTHS

"Everyone understand what they're supposed to do?" I asked in a low voice as we huddled together back in our common room while we were between classes.

We didn't have to go to lunch for another hour, and I was pretty sure both the janitor and the maintenance man would be tied up for at least that long. It had sounded like they had a huge mess to fix and clean up, and this might be our only chance to search their offices.

"This is crazy, you guys. We're going to get caught," Hope whispered, wringing her hands on her apron.

"We're not going to get caught if you stay calm and follow the plan," I said. "You all hang out on the floor and spread out. Some of you in the common room, some in the suites, some in the kitchen, and some in the gym. If our RA's or professors or FBI ask where I am, tell them I'm lying down because I still feel sick. Our rooms and the bathrooms are the only ones not monitored. I mean, we get dressed in there and shower in the bathroom. If they monitored us, that would make them Peeping Toms. Everyone knows that's just wrong, so we should be safe."

"You can't do this alone, Sam," Francesca said, then smiled and shot me a mischievous look as she added, "Take Brent with you. He can search one office while you're searching the other."

My heart lagged and then rebooted loudly in my chest. "But how will we explain his absence?"

"Simple," Brent answered. "I hurt my back in Lab today when Francesca blasted me clear across the room with her blow-dryer ear."

"Hey, it wasn't my fault you got in the way." Francesca crossed her arms on a pout.

"How could I *not* get in the way? You need to learn to control that thing. It felt like an F6 tornado blew through the room. I'm surprised I don't have whiplash. I hit the wall hard. Everyone saw. And Dr. Guggenheim told me to take a long hot shower, so that's what I'll do." He smiled widely. "Or so they'll think."

"Wait a minute," Michaela said. "Girls aren't allowed in the boys' suite, so how am I supposed to make a trapdoor in their bathroom ceiling and cut a hole in the air duct for him to escape out of like I am for you?"

I took a deep breath and thought about this. "You're not. I'll google the instructions on how to do it, and you can just give me one of your tools."

"How?" Michaela looked a little freaked out. "My tools are attached to my body. It would be like amputating an arm or a leg, literally." She took a step back from us.

"She won't have to, Sam," Brent said. "When you escape through your vent, follow the ductwork until you're over the boys' bathroom, then knock. When I hear the knock, I'll win something that can cut through the ceiling and ductwork, and then I'll escape with you. We'll figure out how to hide the hole later."

"It'll have to work. We're running out of time," I said, and then walked off to my suite, moaning and holding my stomach as though I was in agony, all for Big Brother's eyes and ears.

I heard Brent say really loudly that he was headed to the showers because his back was killing him. Then everyone else made plans to play Ping-Pong, work out, or watch TV.

All systems go on Operation Find the Mole!

I paced my bedroom, studying the floor plans for IPR which were mentally stored in my cerebellum. Sector 4, where the janitor and maintenance man were working, was far away from both offices, so Brent and I should be good on sleuthing without interference.

"You ready?" Michaela popped her head in my door.

"Finally. I didn't think you were ever going to show."

"Got held up when Warden Robbins made her rounds. For some reason she was more than happy not to go anywhere near your room."

I laughed. "Because I pretended I was going to throw up on her. That got her to leave me alone in a hurry."

"Good, because you only have an hour." Michaela looked at her watch. "More like fifty-five minutes."

"Then we'd better move it." I pressed my temples, activating my x-ray vision to see where the air duct went through the ceiling. Then I dragged my desk chair into the closet and stood on it. I blinked my eyes to rid them of their double vision so I could use a pencil to draw a square on the sheetrock.

"Cut along those lines," I said as I hopped off. "The closet will be the safest spot to keep a secret hatch."

Michaela pointed her index finger, and a thin-bladed

sheetrock saw slid out of the tip. Stepping on the chair, she was able to reach the ceiling. After sawing along the lines, forming a square big enough for me to crawl through, she popped out that section of sheetrock and handed it to me. "Set it on the dresser. After you're through, I'll fix the hinge so we have a trapdoor in case we need an escape hatch later."

She then chose a different finger and cracked that knuckle. A metal saw slid out of that one. She cut a hole in the air duct and handed me the piece of metal. "Hide that one under your bed, and we'll get rid of the evidence when the coast is clear."

I did as she suggested and returned just as she filed down the edges of the metal so I wouldn't cut myself. "Okay, you're good to go. When you get back, push on the trapdoor and it should pop open. I'll leave the chair in the closet so you don't break your neck climbing down."

"Sounds good. Wish me luck."

"Oh, chica, you're going to need a lot more than luck to pull this one off."

"Gee, thanks."

"Just keeping it real." She saluted me.

I shook my head, wasting no time climbing inside the air duct. Turning on my mental GPS, I set the coordinates for the boys' bathroom. My head tipped, nose twitched, and tongue clicked as my robotic voice spit out the directions, leading the way. Once I was directly over top, I knocked three times.

"Sam? Is that you?" I heard Brent's muffled voice.

*No, it's a really large rat,* I wanted to say. I mean, of course, it was me. Who else would be knocking from inside an air duct? But I took a deep breath to calm my nerves and replied, "Fabsolutely."

I heard him chuckle. "Hang on a second. This will only take a minute."

It took several.

"You sure you know how to tell time?" I hissed, "because my watch shows it's been a whole lot longer than sixty seconds there, Spanky."

"You try playing this game. It's not easy winning all these battles. I'm actually sweating."

"Battles?" That didn't sound good.

"*Yes!*"

I jumped. "Well, you don't have to shout."

"I'm not shouting--I'm winning. Now stand back."

"W-Why?" I sputtered.

"I'm going to cut through the sheetrock and metal now."

"Okay," I said and scooted back, but couldn't help wondering what he'd won in a video game that would cut through both sheetrock and metal.

All of a sudden, a ridiculously long, lethal-looking blade sliced clean through both pieces of material as though it were sinking through a pound of butter.

I stifled a scream. "What is that thing?" I squeaked.

"Excalibur," came his still muffled response.

"Expialidocious? What are you talking about?" I whined. "I'm not Mary Poppins, you know, and this so isn't super-anything."

Within seconds, he'd carved away a circle and the pieces of ceiling fell out. He caught them before they would crash to the tub floor and set off an alarm. I gaped down at him, but he just grinned up at me. "You might not be Mary, but I am definitely 'The King.'"

"You try to dub me, and I swear I'm in just the mood to deck you." I smirked, completely out of patience now. "Enough with the games. We've got some suspects to investigate. And by the way, a square would have been easier for Michaela to make a trapdoor out of," I pointed out.

"Yeah, but a circle was easier for me to cut right now." He hoisted himself through the hole, no chair necessary, and then smiled wide.

Hello, Mr. Adorable!

I almost sighed at the play of muscles in his arms as I watched from a distance. Francesca's blessing for me to date him came back to me full force. But then I remembered Special Agent Crawford's warning that dating a fellow team-mate was not advised, followed quickly by Michaela's reminder that we only had fifty-five minutes. I glanced at my watch.

Correction: fifty minutes!

"Follow me." I turned around and illuminated my cell hand so we could see as we crawled on our hands and knees through the dark, musty air duct. "The offices aren't far apart, so we should be able to stay together until the very end. Once we come to the fork, I'll go left to the janitor's office, and you go right to the maintenance man's."

"What do we do after we're done searching," Brent asked from behind me, and I suddenly realized that he had a full view of my spandex-covered behind. "W-What was the question?" I stuttered, crawling quicker.

"How are we going to get out of the air ducts to search the office? It's not like we have Michaela with us to use her tools. I can probably win another sword or something, but how am I going to cover it up and what are you going to do?"

"I hadn't thought that far ahead." I studied the charts. "Your air duct ends on the floor with a grate in front of it. If you can win something to screw the grate back on, then you're good to go. I'll figure mine out when I'm there. Once you get done searching, go back through the grate all the way to the fork in the air ducts. I'll meet up with you there and lead the way back. Think you can handle that?"

"Yeah, I think so."

"Great, because here's the fork. Good luck."

"You too," he said, and then bumped my behind with his shoulder as he scooted by me and turned right.

I took a minute to watch him crawl, suddenly deciding I loved our uniforms. He peeked over his shoulder and frowned at me. "You okay? You've got a weird look on your face again."

I snapped out of my doofus state. "Yup, I'm fine. Just making sure you knew the way." I turned around and took off as fast as my hands and knees would carry me, my cheeks burning hotly every inch of the way.

Finally, I stopped right over the top of the janitor's office. Following the duct to the floor, it also ended with a grate right in front. But how the heck was I going to get through it? I wasn't Michaela with tools in my hands or Brent who was able to win whatever he needed. Samantha Granger would have to get out of this one, not Digital Diva. I reached into my hair and pulled out the bobby pins I'd stuck in for those pesky pieces of hair that refused to stay in my standard ponytail.

I bent the pin until it looked like the end of a flathead screwdriver and then tried to use it to unscrew the four screws holding the grate in place. Only, I was on the inside of the grate and the screws were on the outside. It wasn't like I was Mr. Fantastic and could stretch my hand through the grate to reach the other side. Frustrated, I shook the grate back and forth hard, and I couldn't believe it when the sheetrock crumbled and the screws broke loose from the wall. Gotta love old buildings, I thought. I glanced at my watch. Man, only thirty minutes left. Pushing the grate out of place, I scrambled out of the air duct, replaced the grate as best I could, and headed straight to the janitor's desk.

Chuck Smith was a slob. Papers everywhere and junk-food wrappers scattered on the floor. Guess since he cleaned up after everyone else all day, he was on strike when it came to himself.

I looked through every item I found and finally came to one piece of paper that had a detective's name written on it. Inspiration struck, and I ran to his filing cabinets. After searching through almost every file, I came to one marked with the detective's name. Pulling the file, I sat down and read it.

The janitor worked days and overtime at night, so he was gone a lot. His wife wanted a lot of improvements made to their home, and she didn't like that he was always working. She was lonely. But lately she hadn't been complaining at all, and whenever he was free, she was missing in action. He suspected she was having an affair. According to the report, the detective had confirmed that, but they still weren't sure who she was seeing.

One thing was obvious. The janitor couldn't have been the guy who had tampered with the bus. He had a receipt, clearly showing why he was late for work the morning the accident had happened. He had been meeting with the detective, paying him for this very report.

I blew out a frustrated breath, hoping Brent had had more luck. After scrambling back into the air duct and wedging the grate back in place, I turned around and made my way to the intersection.

Brent was there waiting for me when I arrived.

"Any luck with the maintenance man?" I asked.

"No, and I almost got caught. I only found receipts for flowers, candy, wine and a hotel room. All on the morning of the accident. I know why Frank Brown was late. He was in a hotel room with some woman."

"How did you almost get caught?"

"Because he came back to his office early, but he wasn't alone. He was with some big lady." Brent shuddered. "I barely made it out before he opened the door."

"What were they doing?"

"You really don't want to know that one. Why do you think I'm back here first?" He looked a little green. "I don't think I'll ever be the same."

I looked at my watch once more. "We'll compare notes later. Right now we'd better hurry. It's almost lunch time, and the last thing we want to do is get caught breaking more rules."

I lit my hand again, the blue-green iridescent light guiding us as we scrambled as fast as we could, taking a detour over the student lounge that was right off the back of the cafeteria. We had almost made it, when I hit a weak spot in the air duct. It creaked and groaned, and I was no longer loving old buildings. I peeked over my shoulder at Brent, my eyes wide.

"Back up," I hissed, but it was too late. The duct and sheetrock gave way below me. I yelped and then reached out and grabbed onto the only thing within reach.

Brent!

We both tumbled, arms around each other, through the ceiling to the floor of the student lounge. Brent broke my fall, and I landed smack dab on top of him. Students, faculty and staff gaped at. We just lay there, staring into each other's eyes, no ESP necessary to know what each other was thinking. Our thoughts were crystal clear.

We were in deep doo-doo now!

## 11

## DETENTION

"Looks like you two are feeling better!" Headmistress Zimmerman said, total shock registering on her face as she looked down at us. "Miss Granger and Mr. Matthews, what in God's name are you doing here--like that?"

I scrambled off of Brent and jumped to my feet as fast I as could. "Um, well, I...we..."

"We both were feeling a lot better, and well, we like each other," Brent blurted, coming to my defense once more as he stood by my side and slipped his arm around me.

"We do," I whispered, staring up at him in wonder.

He ignored me, squeezing my side as he spoke to the Headmistress. "I know we're not supposed to date each other, but we just wanted to spend a little time together so we snuck out."

"Through the air ducts? Do you know how dangerous that could have been, young man?"

"Well, not really because we're--"

"--in a world of trouble," she quickly cut him off with a

stern look, her eyes darting around at all the "normal" IPR students who were glued to the scene.

"Right, sorry," Brent said, looking embarrassed.

"Oh, you *will* be by the time I get through with you. And don't you worry, you'll be spending plenty of time together." She glared at both of us. "In detention!"

My heart sank. My mother was going to go ballistic.

Headmistress Zimmerman led the way past a room labeled "Detention!" and entered her office. "Shut and lock the door behind you, please."

I didn't have a good feeling about this. "Didn't we just pass the normal room you use for detention back there?" I asked.

She turned to us and arched a sleek, pristine-white brow. "Yes we did, but then again, neither of you are normal, now are you?"

I sighed. "Guess not."

"Where are you taking us?" Brent shot me a nervous look.

"The less you know, Mr. Matthews, the better." She turned around and pulled a book off her bookshelf against the back wall. The shelf slid to the right, revealing a secret door with a special keypad. Shielding the keypad from our vision, Headmistress Zimmerman typed in a series of numbers.

Little did she know, that couldn't stop me. I pulled on my ear and recorded an audio of the sounds the numbers made as she punched them in. Then my sensory neurons carried the data into my cerebrum and stored it in a file in my brain to analyze later. I shook my head to get rid of the ringing in my ears and kept watching.

My eyes bugged as a holograph touch pad appeared

before the door, and the Headmistress pressed her thumbprint on the square. A pleasant female voice kind of like my GPS voice echoed out the speakers, saying, "Welcome, Agent Zero."

I stifled a gasp, my eyes locking with Brent's, who looked just as stunned as I felt. Absolutely nothing about this school was normal.

The door slid open, and a dark stairway appeared before us. Headmistress Zimmerman--aka Agent Zero--clapped her hands twice and the hallway flickered to life with the blinding glow of fluorescent lights. We followed behind her down the cement staircase to a room in the basement. There was nothing inside except more fluorescent lights, a table, and a couple chairs. It looked like one of those prison isolation cells you see in the movies. She motioned for us to sit in the chairs, and then she headed for the door.

"Wait! You're just going to leave us here?" I squeaked.

She paused with her hand on the door. "Detention isn't fun, Miss Granger. I suggest you remember that and think twice before you sneak out on any more adventures." And just like that she was gone.

"Well this stinks," Brent said on a huge puff of air. "What are we supposed to do?"

"I have no clue," I answered, plopping my chin on the palm of my hand. We'd really made a mess of things this time.

His face lit up. "I know--we can compare notes."

I held up a finger for him to wait and I scanned the room. Nothing inside, but I was more nervous about what we "couldn't" see. I blinked hard, activating my x-ray vision and looked behind the walls. Oh yeah, big brother was watching and listening to everything we said or did--even way down here.

Blinking my x-ray off, I rubbed the black and white shadows from my eyes as I said, "Sure," a bit louder than I needed to. "You can fill me in on all the notes you took in *Lab* earlier since I missed it." I tapped my eye and pulled on my ear, hoping he'd get the hint.

"Ahhh, okay." Brent nodded slowly and then rubbed his jaw like he was thinking hard. "How about we play a video game first."

"You can't be serious." I frowned. "Don't you think filling me in is a little more important?" I gave him a knowing look. "I really want to make sure I'm up to speed."

"Listen to me." He raised his eyebrows and stared hard at me. "You're going to love this game. It will be worth playing this first. We'll have plenty of time for Lab later."

I knew he was up to something, but I wasn't sure what exactly. Going with my gut, I decided to roll with it. It wasn't like I had many other options. "Okay, fine. So what game are we going to play anyway?"

"Super Smash Brothers. I'll be Luigi," he said slowly and with emphasis, "and you can be Mario."

What was he getting at? I narrowed my eyes. "Isn't that game a little old school?"

"Yeah it's old--kind of like half the *staff* around here. But it has a great story, if you know what I mean."

It suddenly dawned on me he was talking in code. This must be his way of filling me in on what he'd found out about the maintenance man. "Okay, I get it." I nodded and then thought of something. "Isn't The Smash Brothers a Nintendo game? How are we going to play this? You only have an Xbox controller."

"There are some advantages to being a superhero, Sam." He beamed. "I'll just download a game demo from the virtual gamer store and use my built-in converter to change the format to Xbox."

"Wow, that's really cool. It's like having all game systems built into one. But what about me?"

He thought for a minute. "I've got it. It's like upstairs with that see-through thingy."

"You mean the holograph touch pad?"

"Yeah, like the one you shot out your eyes that time in Lab. Can you make a holograph TV screen?"

"Let me check." I closed my eyes and searched the instruction manual in my forebrain, taking forever to find what I was looking for. Navigating that massive book hadn't gotten any easier. I opened my eyes, my temples throbbing from straining my brain. "Yeah, I should be able to, but what about...you know."

"We're not playing Xbox Live, so we won't be communicating with the outside world or breaking any rules. We're just playing a video game with each other, so I don't see anything wrong with that. And hey, it's good practice of our powers."

I shrugged. "Okay, here goes." I concentrated hard, and out popped a holograph through the pupils of my eyes in the shape of a large, plasma flat-screen TV. "Now what?" I asked, ignoring the burn. My eyes would be dilated for a week after we were done.

"Awesome!" Brent stared in awe. "Can you add a virtual keyboard?"

"Sure." I waved my hand in front of me, and a holograph of a virtual keyboard appeared as though floating on air. I felt like Ironman and had to admit this was pretty cool.

Brent fused his hands together into an Xbox controller, started up the video game demo, and then hit pause. "Okay, now tap into my system and link up with me. We will be the only two playing this game."

"I'll try." I fired up my cell hand, squeezed a fist, and then flung it open to shoot a pulse through cyberspace. It hit its target, intercepting Brent's Xbox signal and tapping into the game he was playing. "It worked, I think."

"Let me test it." He took the game off pause, and Mario and Luigi appeared larger than life on my holograph TV, in HD no less. Blue overalls, red and blue hats, matching mustaches, and a castle looming before them in the distance. "Cool. Now follow my lead," he added.

"Wait, which one are you?"

"I'm Luigi. You're Mario. Understand?" His gaze locked on mine.

I nodded. Then that meant Mario was the janitor and Luigi was the maintenance man. "So what now?"

"Um, well, what do you know about Mario?" He asked as he started moving his character toward the castle.

"That he always has to rescue Princess Peach because she is constantly getting into trouble." It just hit me. This would be the perfect scenario to fill Brent in, too. "Yeah, that's right. She's not as innocent as she seems," I said with more enthusiasm, jumping over and fighting off various animals that were trying to block my path. "Mario really likes Princess Peach and he thought she liked him back, but she just might like someone else more than him. Like maybe Bowser the ten-foot evil turtle has finally won Princess Peach's heart."

"Really?" Brent's character battled another animal, trying to catch up to my guy who was kicking butt and taking names.

"Yeah. I think that's what Mario is afraid of." My fingers

flew over my virtual keyboard as I started scaling the castle wall.

"Hmmm, then maybe he caused a little trouble himself?" Brent asked, glancing at me quickly before following my lead up the side of the castle.

"Nope, couldn't have." I sighed. "He was busy confirming his suspicions about Princess Peach and trying to rescue her from getting herself into more trouble."

"That stinks." Brent looked around the room. "I mean, it stinks that I just got knocked down off the castle." His thumbs maneuvered the knobs on his controller hands and his character scrambled up the side of the castle wall, trying to catch up to mine again.

"What about Luigi?" I asked, falling behind his character now. I had to admit Brent was good. We could see Princess Peach standing in the window in her pink dress, white gloves and shiny blond hair. "Isn't Luigi always helping Mario?"

"Yeah, but he's not as *good* as Mario." Brent's eyes darted to mine and then back at my holograph TV screen. "I think he causes as much trouble as Princess Peach if you know what I mean."

"Like super-big trouble?" Hope blossomed in my chest.

"More like super-naughty trouble, but not so much super-big." Brent frowned. "Let's just say he's not the bomb."

"Oh." My hopes of having caught our bad guy evaporated. All we'd discovered were the staff's secrets, but nothing to prove any one of them was our bad guy. Guess that meant we were back to Square One.

"It doesn't look like we're any closer to taking down the evil turtle, Bowser. I haven't seen a single sign of him. I guess we'd better get to work on those Lab notes." Brent shut down the game, his shoulders slumping.

I swiped away my virtual keyboard and closed my eyes, turning off the holograph TV. Blinking them open, I rubbed the sting from them. "We'll go over the notes in a minute, but first..." I thought of Francesca and all her courage. If Brent and I were going to stand a chance, I had to get closer to him. Learn more about him.

"What?" he asked, eyeing me curiously.

"Well, it's just...you know so much about me, but I feel like I hardly know you." I pressed my lips together and waited.

"What do you want to know?"

I bit my bottom lip. "Everything."

"Okay, but after that phone call with your friend Mel, I have some questions, too."

"Deal." I smiled shyly and listened.

Brent talked about his family and his ex-girlfriend. He really opened up about how being a superhero had affected his life. I found myself telling him all about Trevor asking someone else to the dance and Mel's ex-boyfriend being a doofus and poor Simon's missing uncle, and even my mom and dad. I still couldn't believe she was dating Trevor's dad. Not that Sheriff Hamilton wasn't totally awesome, but I still had hopes my mom would get back together with my dad.

Our time in detention brought us closer somehow, and Brent was so easy to talk to. For the first time, I wondered if maybe we really did stand a chance at having a relationship. Until I found a way to reverse what had happened to us, he was as close to dating as I was ever going to get.

A little while later Headmistress Zimmerman whipped open the door as though trying to catch us in the act of doing something wrong. But we were done playing our video game and done getting to know each other better. Now we really were studying, looking like the perfect students, even though we both felt like we'd failed at this mission today.

"Detention is over," she snapped. "Time to go back to your dorms." She didn't look happy, but there was nothing she could do about it. After all, we hadn't broken any rules.

Now if we could just figure out what it all meant...

## THREE STRIKES: YOU'RE OUT!

We sat in the cafeteria at a special table for dinner that night. Special Agent Crawford had been watching us like a hawk after the "falling through the air duct" incident that Headmistress Zimmerman had told her about. Alice Little, the lunch lady, motioned the agent over. With one last narrow-eyed look in our direction that screamed, *behave yourselves or else*, Special Agent Crawford marched over to the cash register with a no-nonsense stride.

Here was our chance.

I waved my hand for everyone to lean in. At least here we were in public around the other "normal" IPR students. No cameras or microphones were close enough for Big Brother to hear.

"Well, what's the deal?" Kyle asked, cracking the knuckles on his cable hand. "Did you find our guy or what?"

"Not exactly," I answered.

"What does that mean?" Amy rubbed her rumbling stomach, which we all knew by now wasn't from hunger. She ate more than anyone I'd ever seen to try to fill her bottomless pit, but nothing ever worked. The only thing in there was loads of sports equipment.

"It means we found out juicy gossip, just nothing we can use to pin the crimes on any of our suspects," I answered.

"Ohhh, dish." Francesca's eyes changed from a pale amber to a bright sparkling turquoise. "I love juicy gossip."

"Well, we all know the janitor was late for work the morning of our field trip, so he could have possibly tampered with the bus," I said. "Only, when I snuck into his office, I found out he had been meeting with a private detective at that time. He thinks his wife is having an affair, and this detective confirmed it. The janitor still doesn't know who the affair is with, but he definitely wasn't the one who blew up the bus."

"Too bad he didn't have my powers," Gi said. "I'd blast her butt if I were Mr. Smith. He's such a nice guy. He really doesn't deserve what his wife is putting him through. I'm glad he's not our guy, because nice or not, I would have blasted him myself if he was. I'm sick of looking over my shoulder."

"That's your problem, you shoot first talk later," Ricky said, his voice cracking on a B-flat.

"Yeah, well, at least I don't skip a beat under pressure." Gi slapped her thighs in a one-two beat, smacking his forehead on three. "Ba-deep, ba-deep...I'm on all night, folks."

"Ha, ha. Real funny." Ricky swiped Gi's hand away. "Anyway, what about the maintenance man, Mr. Brown? He's still a suspect, isn't he?"

"Um, not exactly," Brent said. "Seems he was hooking up with some woman the morning of the accident. That's why he was late."

"What are you saying, dude, we have no suspects?"

Warren asked, mouth hanging open, looking totally confused.

"You seriously have rubber for a brain," Michaela chimed in on an eye roll.

"Yeah, well you're full of nuts and bolts, baby. It's time you loosened up a little."

"All right, you two. Save the flirting for some other time," Hope said. "Keep it clean. We have work to do."

"That's right, Hope." Parker grinned widely at her, bright red roses blossoming on his cheeks. "We need to focus on finding the mole."

"And we will," said Brent. "Just because the janitor and maintenance man have alibis doesn't mean the lunch lady is off the hook. We still don't know why she looks so upset lately."

"You're a genius, Brent," I said, and he puffed out his chest, looking pleased. "I think we need to look into her tomorrow. Maybe we can search the files we saw in Head-mistress Zimmerman's office."

"But we can't leave our private wing on our own," Francesca said. "There's only one way into her office, and it's right on the main floor. Someone will see us for sure if we sneak out."

Brent and I looked at each other, obviously thinking the same thoughts as he said, "Believe me, there's another way in. We'll just have to wait for a sign that the time is right."

THE NEXT MORNING, SIR LANCELOT SAUNTERED INTO OUR common room looking worried.

"Lance, what's wrong?" I asked.

"Professor Westcott was parking her car for this morning's classes when the snowplow the groundskeeper, Mr. Price, was driving crashed into her."

"Oh no, is she okay?" Francesca asked.

"She's fine," Warden Robbins answered, rolling her eyes. "A broken collarbone and a few broken ribs. Big whoop. I've had worse," she said. "Everyone's acting like it's the end of the world. I just want to get to the good stuff. This program is taking much longer than I expected, and I'm getting bored. At least now that they're short-handed, maybe they'll let us help. Give us some real work to do."

We all gaped at her.

"What's been happening around here *is* a big deal, Tracy." Lance shook his head at her. "This is the third professor involved in this program who's gotten hurt. Who's next--Dr. Guggenheim? And then what--the students? Us?" He took a deep breath. "What if someone dies next time? This whole thing is getting out of hand. I'm going to go see what I can find out." He stood and headed for the elevators.

"Whatever." She huffed. "That's right--you go be the favorite. I'll just do your job, too, and baby-sit the whole floor," she yelled after him sarcastically, but he ignored her and kept walking. She stomped her foot and then turned on us. "Any of you little twerps steps out of line, some heads are gonna roll." Then she stormed off to her room.

"What's the plan, Sam?" Brent asked in a low voice.

"I stayed up, thinking about this all last night," I answered. "This is what I came up with. Warren, you stay in the boys' suite practicing your BMX skills down the hallway. You're our eyes and ears for the boys. And Gi, you stay in our end doing your target practice down the hallway. You're our eyes and ears there. Got it?"

They both nodded.

"Ricky and Parker, you take the hallway by the elevator

and have a battle-of-the-artists competition. Music versus art. Winner gets to hold a concert or festival in the common room with all of us attending."

Ricky and Parker perked up while everyone else grumbled.

"I think it's a great idea," Hope said. "And it's only fair we support each other. We're a team, remember?"

"Amy, you take the gym. Get your workout in early. Will that work for you?" I asked.

She nodded.

"Good. Hope, you take the kitchen. It's a mess, so I'm sure you'll have plenty to keep you busy."

Hope's eyes sparkled.

"Francesca, you can take the game room. Do your nails and makeup at the card table or something. And Kyle, you get the couch, of course. Now I just have to figure out how to get Brent and I into the secret stairwell that leads to Headmistress Zimmerman's office."

"What about Agent Zero?" Brent asked.

"After the accident happened this morning, I turned on my super-sonic hearing and heard them call an emergency staff meeting which started..." I glanced at my watch, "ten minutes ago. Her office will be empty for a while, so Brent and I should be good to scan the files for the lunch lady and the groundskeeper. His snowplow ran into Professor Westcott's car, and I heard them say the brake line was cut. Looks like the accident wasn't an accident this time either."

"Well, we can't go through the air ducts again," Brent said while pacing, but then he stopped and looked up. "Isn't the detention room on the other side of the gym wall?"

I closed my eyes, the gears churning as I pulled up the floor plans in my mind's eye. After studying them, I opened my eyes, a slight headache lingering as I said, "Hey, you're right. It is. But how are we going to get there, short of blasting a hole through the wall? I don't think we can hide that as easy as a hole in the ceiling."

"We don't need a hole." Brent rubbed his jaw, thinking. "Yeah, that will work. You just need to hold my hand."

I looked around at everyone staring at us both funny. Leaning forward, I whispered, "Um, okay, but right here in front of everyone?"

"Yeah, but in just a sec." Brent seemed oblivious to my discomfort as he turned to Kyle. "When I give you the signal, pause the cameras and count to ten, then turn them back on. After fifteen minutes exactly, pause the cameras and count to ten again. Think you can handle that?"

"In my sleep," said the king.

"Good. Okay, places everyone," Brent said, and when everyone went to their designated spots, he started playing a video game.

I just stood there watching him, pretending to be into the video game. It was some paranormal ghost-zombie-vampire game. It was actually kind of cool and I got totally into it for real, almost forgetting why he was playing, when he said, "*Yes!*" and fist-pumped the air.

Kyle took that as his signal and hit pause on his remote-control hand, which he'd aimed at the cameras. Then he started counting. Brent grabbed my hand and a jolt of electricity raced up my arm, but then he yanked me with him and started running for the wall.

"Hey, wait! We're going too fast. This is crazy. What are you doing? We're going to hit the wall!" I shrieked.

Brent ignored me and picked up speed. I held out my free hand and closed my eyes on a scream. Instead of the impact of solid wall smashing into my face, I felt almost weightless. My legs still pumped as I pried open my eyes and stared in shock. We had passed right through the common-room wall, into the gym, and straight through to the detention room. Panting and out of breath, we stopped in front of the door to the stairway.

"We've got to hurry before the cameras come on," Brent said. "I got us inside the detention room, but how are you going to get us into the stairwell? The wall is made of solid steel, and I can't pass us through that."

I thought a minute and then grinned up at him. "You're not the only one with tricks up your sleeve." I pressed on my earlobe and played the audio I'd recorded of Headmistress Zimmerman, punching in the code to bring up the holograph. My computer brain analyzed the sounds and computed a set of numbers in my mind's eye. I punched in the numbers and the same holograph with the touch pad Headmistress Zimmerman had used appeared before us.

"Okay, genius, what about Headmistress Zimmerman's thumbprint?"

"No worries. I had Hope snag the Headmistress's glass at dinner last night. Parker lifted the print, reproduced it on his stomach canvas, and then tattooed a copy onto my thumb."

Brent's eyes bugged. "Won't your parents kill you for getting a tattoo?"

"It's not permanent--it's a henna tattoo. But we've got to hurry. We only have fifteen minutes to search that office before Kyle turns the cameras off again. Let's just hope this works." I held my breath as I pressed my thumb onto the virtual keypad and the door opened.

We ran into the stair case, the door closing behind us, and then everything turned pitch black. I reached out but only felt something solid. Brent's chest. I almost sighed, keeping my hands flattened across his muscles.

"Um, Sam?" I could hear him breathe.

"Yeah?" I sounded just as breathless.

"That's not the wall."

I jerked my hands back. "Oh, sorry." Then I remembered what Headmistress Zimmerman had done. Clapping my hands twice, I watched the hallway flicker to life with fluorescent lights. I darted past Brent, too embarrassed to look in his eyes. Besides, we had a job to do. No time for distractions of that kind.

Opening the door to the Headmistress's office, I chewed the inside of my cheek and hoped everyone was still in their meeting. When the door swung open wide to reveal an empty office, relief filled me. "Okay, I'll take this filing cabinet and you search her desk," I said to Brent.

"Aye, aye, Captain." He saluted me and then got to work.

Ten minutes later, I found Alice Little's file. "No wonder she's been so upset lately."

"What happened?" Brent asked.

"It says she's on probation. At risk of losing her job because she got caught fraternizing with a fellow employee. I guess that's not allowed, especially since it's been affecting her work." I gasped. "Oh, my gosh, it gets worse. She's the big lady you saw the maintenance man, Mr. Brown, with. Holy cow, you're not going to believe this." I looked up at him. "Her last name might be Little, but she's married. She's the wife of Mr. Smith, the janitor."

"Seriously?" Brent looked stunned. "What a mess, but at least we know one thing. She can't be our bad guy if she was the one in that hotel room with Mr. Brown that morning."

"Wow," I said, feeling bad for Mr. Smith. "Who would have thought the evil turtle Bowser wasn't the bad guy after all. Poor Mario never expected someone as close to him as Luigi would be the one causing all the 'trouble' with Princess Peach."

"Forget that--who would have thought Alice Little was Princess Peach." Brent looked as shocked as I felt.

"Did you find anything on the groundskeeper, Mr. Price?"

"Yeah, there's a report on the desk that says Mr. Price's son was denied admittance into IPR because he wasn't special enough." Brent's eyes locked onto mine. "I guess Professor Westcott was the one who said no. She refused to recommend him, and Mr. Price has hated her ever since."

"Yeah, but enough to try to kill her?" I asked.

"Maybe. We know he had motive, but we just don't know if he has an alibi."

Footsteps sounded outside the door and a lock jiggled the key. Brent and I scrambled over to the bookcase and were just about to pull the book that opened the secret door when the office door swung open.

Busted!

Headmistress Zimmerman, Special Agent Crawford, and Agent Maxwell stared at us, pure shock registering on their faces. The shock disappeared and anger quickly took its place. Even someone as crafty as Brent couldn't come up with a story convincing enough to get us off the hook this time. My parents always say honesty is the best policy.

I decided we had nothing to lose.

Brent started to say something, but I put my hand on his shoulder and stepped forward. Looking each of them in the eye, I put on my serious face and simply said, "We need to talk."

# 13

# THE ACCUSED

Turns out my parents were right. Being honest totally paid off. I told the FBI and the Head-mistress everything we'd found. That, along with the evidence they had collected, had been enough to arrest the groundskeeper, Mr. Price, for committing attempted murder on Professor Westcott. They didn't have enough to link him to the other "accidents" on Professor Troubadour and Professor Hillcrest, but everyone was confident he was the mole we were after.

A week had gone by and pretty much everything had been smooth sailing. We all felt safe and classes had resumed--until today.

We now sat in the same auditorium like we had that first morning we'd been introduced to the program. Sir Lancelot sat at the end of our row, but there was no sign of Warden Robbins. In fact, none of us had seen her all morning, which was fine with me.

Dr. Guggenheim stood beside Headmistress Zimmerman on one side of the podium, with Special Agent Crawford and Agent Maxwell on the other. All four were discussing something serious, according to the expressions on their faces. Finally, Dr. Guggenheim stepped up to the microphone.

"Good morning, boys and girls. You're all probably wondering why we didn't have class this morning. Unfortunately, the police had to let Mr. Price go. They didn't have enough hard evidence to convict him of the attempts on your professor's lives. They are afraid the real culprit is still at large.

"If the FBI can't guarantee your safety or mine, then we are left with no choice but to cancel the program," he shot them a hard look, "even though it breaks my heart to do so." He looked back at us and smiled sadly. "If only we could catch the real culprit, then maybe we wouldn't have to leave."

The microphone in his hand started sparking, and he let out a little yelp, throwing it away from himself and the other people onstage. It hit the ground, rolled, and set the curtains to the stage on fire. Alarms screeched, and chaos erupted.

Dr. Guggenheim sprang into action like a true hero. "Follow me, boys and girls. Quickly, now. Stay calm, and everything will be all right." We felt safe with him. He made sure we all reached the door through the thickening smoke while the FBI agents put out the fire.

He led us all the way back to our dorms. When we got off the elevator, Warden Robbins stood staring at us, looking weird. Not to mention, she looked awful with messy hair, red-rimmed eyes, and a spacey look on her face.

"Tracy, where have you been," Dr. Guggenheim said, frowning as he took in her appearance. "Lance said you weren't in your room this morning, and you never showed up at the assembly. You have some explaining to do, young lady."

"I would..." she rubbed her eyes and scratched her head, "if I could remember."

"Have you been drinking?" He looked shocked.

"I'm eighteen, not an idiot, sir." She scowled.

He leaned forward and sniffed. "It's obvious you've been doing something."

"This program is bogus anyway. I haven't done anything exciting since I started, and now you're accusing me?" She started to leave. "I don't have to take this. I quit."

Dr. Guggenheim grabbed her arm. "Oh, you're not going anywhere until we clear all this up. Lance, call Special Agent Crawford up here this instant."

Tracy tugged, but Dr. Guggenheim was stronger than he looked. Her eyes darted around a bit wildly now. "What are you doing? You're all crazy."

"Are we? Or is that just the paranoia of getting caught setting in?" The doctor studied her eyes and pursed his lips, the frown between his brows deepening.

"Getting caught doing what? I didn't do anything, I swear," Tracy said, sounding like a scared little girl and not much like the bully warden she had been. I actually felt sorry for her.

"Then by all means, child. Tell us where you were all morning?"

"I—I don't know. I'm telling you the truth, I really don't remember."

"Likely story." He tsked and then turned to all of us. "This is exactly why you should stay in school and stay out of trouble." He looked back at her. "That little stunt you pulled could have killed me."

"I'm telling you I didn't do anything," she wailed.

"I'll be the judge of that," Special Agent Crawford said as she stepped off the elevator. She stopped beside Dr.

Guggenheim and studied Tracy closely. Then said to the doctor, "We found this small, gold stud earring by the fuse box." She leaned to the side and looked at Tracy's ears. "Exactly like the one she's wearing. Funny how your other earring hole is empty."

Tracy's eyes widened and she reached up to touch the empty hole, looking dazed and confused.

Special Agent Crawford continued, "We also found fingerprints on the faulty chord to the microphone. We're analyzing them now, but my guess is we'll find a match to her. I think we've found our criminal."

"C-Criminal...." Tracy sobbed, looking truly upset. "I couldn't have, could I?"

"If I remember right, you don't get paid if you quit," Dr. Guggenheim said. "Maybe forcing the program to get canceled was your out. Lance told me how you said the program was stupid anyway." The doctor shook his head sadly. "Such a shame. You had loads of potential, Miss Robbins. You would have made a fine scientist."

Special Agent Crawford led a crying Tracy Robbins out the door, who just kept repeating, "I swear I don't remember doing anything. I'm so sorry."

Dr. Guggenheim turned to us, looking serious. "I'm sorry you all had to see that, just take it as a lesson of what not to do. On a positive note, at least we can resume classes. I expect to see you all first thing in the morning at Lab. Get some sleep and be on time, ready to work."

---

"DID YOU HEAR THE NEWS?" FRANCESCA SAID IN LAB THE next morning.

"What are you talking about?" I asked.

"Today's our last day of class, dude," Warren said, stealing Francesca's thunder.

She scowled and finished before he could, "The program is still being cancelled."

A rumble of confusion sounded throughout the room. Dr. Guggenheim still hadn't arrived, and we were all getting antsy. I hoped something bad didn't happen to him.

"Wait. I heard Tracy's fingerprints were a match," Michaela said. "They arrested her and because she's eighteen, she can be tried as an adult I guess. Can you imagine? I mean, there aren't a set of iron bars I couldn't cut my way out of, but Tracy, not so much. She's just a normal person."

"I know, right?" Gi said. "I always knew she was kind of tough and mean, and I sometimes wondered if she took steroids from the size of her and her mood swings, but I never thought she was capable of trying to kill someone."

"It doesn't make sense, though," Brent said. "If they know who was behind all the crazy stuff that happened around here, then why is the program being cancelled still?"

"I heard they can't link her to all the other accidents for sure, and the FBI doesn't want to take any more chances," Kyle added on a shrug. "I don't really care anymore. I'm ready to get back to normal."

"I don't think any of us will ever be truly normal again," Hope said on a sigh.

"Sorry I'm late," Dr. Guggenheim stated as he strolled into our classroom and set a stack of books and folders on his desk. He paced, rubbing his brow, and then finally faced us. "I apologize for failing you all."

"You didn't fail us," Ricky said.

"Yes," the doctor nodded gravely, "Yes, I did. This program was supposed to help you get a handle on your wonderful abilities. Oh, I know the government had their own plans for you to be an elite group of superheroes, but it's wrong for them to use you for their own purposes. They can't see how truly special you all are, and now we'll never fully know the extent of what you can do. I just wish we'd had a little more time for me to help you."

"But you've helped us in so many ways," Amy said. "It's because of you we're actually a team now."

"Yeah. I didn't know half of what I was capable of before I came here," Parker added, glancing at Hope. "Or what to do with it."

"Thank you, boys and girls. That really means a lot to me. I did my best to get them to change their mind, but they wouldn't listen. Unfortunately, it's all over now." Dr. Guggenheim's face fell in defeat.

The loudspeakers came on, interrupting all the classrooms. Headmistress Zimmerman's voice rang out loud and clear with a bit of a tremble. "Can I have your attention everyone? Please exit the building immediately in a calm, orderly fashion. There has been a bomb threat, and we need to evacuate the building at once. I repeat, please leave the building right now."

We all jumped up and started running for the door.

"Whoa, whoa. Calm down and just relax for a minute," Dr. Guggenheim said, holding up his hands and blocking our way out. "We certainly don't want anyone else to get hurt, now do we? The halls are going to be swamped, so if we just sit tight for a minute, we'll be better off."

Just as he'd said, the sounds of rushing footsteps and shouts of terror filled the hallway outside. We waited a good ten minutes until things quieted down, and then Dr. Guggenheim tried the door.

It didn't open.

He tried it again, without luck, and then turned to face

us. "Um, I'm not sure why, but the door seems to be stuck." He frowned. "There must be a logical explanation, but in the meantime, let's look for another way out."

"But there *is* no other way out. This wing was designed to keep us in!" Hope fairly shouted, wringing her apron with her hands. "What if there is a real bomb? What if it goes off before we escape? I don't want to die."

"I'm here for you," Parker said, stepping to her side. "I don't know what we can do, but we'll do it together." He took her hand in his and a flower blossomed on the back of his skin and then crept like a vine across his fingers until it transferred to her hand. She reached her scrubber palm up, ready to scour it off out of instinct, but then made a fist like she was trying to resist the urge. She succeeded and left the tattoo on her skin while blinking back tears.

"It's going to take the FBI a while to make sure every student is accounted for outside. They might not even know we're still in the building yet," Francesca said, highlights and lowlights alternating throughout her hair in Technicolor as her nerves took over.

"Yeah, and these walls are a foot thick. It's not like I can shoot our way out." Gi flipped the safety on her gun hands, and her shoulders slumped as a hopeless look crossed her face.

"I can play you a song if it will make you feel better," Ricky said.

Gi just stared at him with a funny expression, but she didn't make a scathing comeback like usual. "Know any pop?" she finally asked.

Ricky smiled fully. "I think I can manage that." Then he began to play a really cool song.

"Nice," Gi said, bobbing her head to the beat.

"Maybe we can drill our way out," Michaela added.

"Through steel? Whoa, dudette, you're my hero." Warren stared at her with an awestruck expression on his face.

"Steel? Oh." Michaela's face fell. "Never mind."

Warren nudged her in the shoulder with his. "You're still my hero."

She just laughed softly and shook her head. "And you're still a dork," she said, but there was no heat to her words, just a hint of humor.

"Wait, I have an idea," Kyle commented, hitting a button on his cell hand. Nothing happened. His face registered shock. He tried again, but still nothing happened. "I don't understand? Why isn't the repeat function working?"

"You can't control everything, Kyle." Amy put her hand on his shoulder, her words gentle.

He stared at her, looking lost.

"It's okay," she said. "You tried."

"But I failed. I'm not used to losing."

"Me either," she said softly, and a new understanding passed between them.

"I guess that's it then." Brent's eyes locked onto mine. "We're doomed."

Just then a noise sounded from outside our door. The lock jiggled, and then the door swung open, revealing Sir Lancelot in all his glory. We all gasped, and you could feel the relief sweep through the room like an antivirus program through an infected computer.

We had just been saved.

## 14

---

## EXPOSED

"Come on. Follow me. Hurry," Lance said, ushering us outside the classroom and into the empty hall, the sirens from outside wailing louder.

"How did you know we were still in here," Dr. Guggenheim sputtered as he brought up the rear.

"Lucky guess," Lance answered as he gave him a funny look. "I'll explain later." He turned down a hallway we'd never been.

"Hey, this isn't the way outside," I said.

"The other way is blocked. You're just going to have to trust me," he responded, and I did. I trusted him completely. He was Sir Lancelot, after all.

After rounding yet another hall, we all passed through a doorway into a large fully equipped lab. Stopping short, we whipped around just as the door slammed shut and locked.

Sirens within the school started screeching even louder than the sirens from the bomb squad outside. I closed my eyes to do a computer scan of the entire building, but nothing worked. I couldn't see anything. I couldn't do anything. Oh, my God, I didn't have any powers! I might have wished for that before, but so not at this moment. I opened my eyes. "What's happening?"

"The school is completely locked down," Lance said. "And you're all my prisoners."

I sucked in a huge breath. Lance? No way!

"What are you saying, young man? Surely you don't mean this?" Dr. Guggenheim said.

Lance stared at him, stunned and then angry. "What am I saying? What are *you* saying? This was your plan."

"My plan? Boy, you've gone mad."

"Oh, no." Lance started waving his hands in front of him. "You're not setting me up like you did Tracy." He turned around and grabbed the door, but Dr. Guggenheim pulled out a gun and knocked him over the head. Lance crumpled to the floor in a heap.

My heart thundered in my chest like a stereo system on high. First Lance and now the doctor? The two people I'd thought most heroic throughout this whole crazy adventure were really the bad guys behind all the accidents. But why?

Dr. Guggenheim turned to us, looking every inch the mad scientist.

"W-Who are you?" I asked on barely more than a whisper.

"I'm disappointed in you, Samantha. I thought for sure you'd figure it out by now." His German accent had disappeared, and his voice sounded oddly familiar.

If I still had my powers, I would process the pitch and tone of his vocal chords. Then my brain would scroll through thousands of mental photographs of people I'd met throughout my life until it locked on a match. But without powers, I was just plain ole Sam.

Only Sam was still a smart girl. I could do this. I just had to think hard. Where had I heard that voice before? All I could think of was it sort of sounded like Simon. But how could that be? I studied the doctor with his thick, dark hair and coke-bottle glasses--thick dark hair that looked like Mom's throw rug, coke-bottle glasses that were probably fake...

I squinted my eyes and studied his features, ignoring the wig and glasses. A picture of a tall, gangly man with russet-colored hair and tawny eyes appeared in my memory. I knew that face. Where had I seen that face?

I stumbled back a couple steps and stared in disbelief as my eyes locked with the madman before me. "You're Simon's missing uncle. The physicist who gave the seminar on electromagnetic fields and energy force fields at Blue Lake University a few months ago."

"Very good, Miss Granger. I'll give you a B considering you're rather late in drawing that conclusion," he said, peeling off his thick, black wig, mustache, and coke-bottle glasses.

I heard rumbles of shock from behind me, but no one dared move. The man we'd trusted the most had betrayed us all.

"In my defense, you were wearing a disguise," I pointed out, stalling and trying to figure out what to do. "Simon is really worried, you know."

The doctor blinked, and a fond look crossed his features. "He always was a good boy."

"Yeah, well, you're not a very good uncle. He's going to be crushed when he finds out what you've done. It's not too late to turn yourself in."

Van Alstyne's face turned hard once more. "Oh, but he won't find out." A crazed look came into his eyes. "No one will."

"How is that possible?" Brent spoke up from beside me.

"You'll see," the doctor said, adding, "By the way, this is my special lab. I've been preparing this room since the day I got here. If you try to communicate with the outside, it won't work. The whole place is rigged to counter all your powers. Within these four walls, you're no longer superheroes." He pointed to a box in the corner of the ceiling that was humming softly. "Remember, no one knows you all better than I do."

He fired up his cell phone and dialed a number as he stepped outside the door, but we could hear everything he said.

"Special Agent Crawford? Oh, thank God, it's you," Simon's uncle said in his fake Dr. Guggenheim voice. "It's Lance. The boy's gone crazy. He's the one behind this whole thing. He's kidnapped the Phenoteens and myself, locking down the entire school. He said he had the place rigged to blow. Please don't try anything crazy. He has a gun. We're okay, but I'm going to try to stop him. Oh no, he's coming! I've got to go."

The doctor came back into the room and relocked the door.

"Is there even a real Dr. Guggenheim?" I asked.

"Of course."

I could feel my face pale, and I swallowed hard, my throat as dry as a printer with no ink. "Then...where is he?"

"When they passed on my grant, I was devastated. My passion has always been fusion. I've never stopped believing when two highly charged objects collide under the right circumstances, one object will absorb the energy of the other.

"Digital Diva was my hope of finally proving my theory." His face turned hard. "But after she disappeared, I became the laughingstock among my peers." His eyes locked onto mine, and I could feel the hatred. "Can you imagine what that did to me?

He began to pace. "When I heard about this special class, I kidnapped the real Dr. Guggenheim and stole his identity. He's in a safe place with my assistant watching over him. I swear that woman would do anything for me. And no one has bothered to look for him because no one knows he's missing. Why would they?" He smiled evilly. "They all think I'm him."

"I don't get why you need us," I said. "Let us go, and we promise we won't turn you in."

"My silly little girl. Now that I've found you, you're not going anywhere. You see when I first started this, I was simply hoping for a glimpse of the infamous Digital Diva. Imagine my surprise when I found out you were her. Even better, that you weren't alone. Just think what I could do with *all* of your abilities. Why I'd be the most powerful person on earth."

*Mwa-ha-ha-ha-haaa* rang silently through my head. The man really was crazy. "All of our powers? What are you talking about?"

"The grand finale, child. My life's work."

"What does that mean?" Brent dared to ask while everyone else was still numb with shock.

"Why, that you will die, and I will become all of you combined, my boy. The world isn't big enough for more than one superhero--for more than one super-me!"

"OH, MY GOD, HE'S INSANE," I SAID, PACING THE LAB WE WERE locked in. Simon Van Alstyne, The First, had stepped out to prepare for his grand transformation.

"Sam, it's okay," Brent said.

"It's not okay. He's going to harness our powers, kill us, and then come off looking like an innocent victim. The only survivor." I stared at Brent in dismay. "He's going to win."

"Calm down. You have to pull it together. We need you." Brent tried to get me to stop, but I dodged him and kept moving back and forth.

"We have no powers. I can't calm down. I can't think. I can't do anything. I'm no leader. I'm a failure. I--"

Brent grabbed my shoulders, stopping me in my tracks, and then swooped down and kissed me hard on the lips. All thoughts fled my brain except one: Mr. Adorable was finally kissing me. So why weren't there any fireworks? No tingles, no curling toes, no nothing. His kiss softened, and then finally he pulled away. We both stared at each other with a look of surprise.

"You feel anything?" I asked, biting my bottom lip.

"Not a thing. You?" he asked, studying me curiously.

"Nope." How did I say this without hurting him? "It, um, was like kissing my brother if I had one."

"Me, too." He looked relieved. "I mean, not my brother, but definitely a sister. Weird."

We both laughed.

"At least now we know," I said.

"Yeah." He smiled. "Friends?"

I smiled back. "The best."

"You better now?"

"I'm more than better--I'm fabulastic. Thanks for that." I took a breath. "Let's go get the others. We need a plan."

"Welcome back, Captain."

The doctor came back into the lab wearing a white lab coat and carrying a clipboard in one hand and a gun in the other. He motioned us to the center of the room. When he pressed a button on a remote control, a false bottom in the floor before us slid open, revealing a metal riser. Each of our names was labeled around the edge of the circular platform.

"Take your spots and stand on your names," he ordered.

Without powers, we had no choice but to do what he said. We all stepped onto the platform. Once we were in place, he hit a button on his remote control, and a compartment in front of each of us opened.

"Pick up the metal chain before you, and clamp the ring around your waist."

We each eyed each other and again did as we were told, but that didn't mean my brain wasn't searching for a way out of this mess. The long metal chain was attached to the platform and the metal ring was attached to the chain, binding us to the contraption like dogs on leashes.

Once we were all secured, the doctor hit another button. Metal poles with tops like the inside of a light bulb raised up out of the floor before each of us, just out of reach. They looked scary, and I couldn't help letting fear consume me.

I took a deep breath, pushed down my fear, and kept it together. If we could just find a way to turn off the box in the corner, we would have our powers back. We weren't smarter than the doctor and could never beat him on our own, but if we worked as a team, we stood a chance.

"What are you going to do to us?" I asked, stalling.

"Ever curious, aren't you Miss Granger?" He hit another button, and up through the floor before him came a bigger version of the meteorite I'd touched back in Blue Lake. "I suppose it doesn't matter that you know since you all will die in the end," he went on.

"When I turn on the simulated meteorite I created, the metal poles before you will act as lightning rods. They will conduct electricity, harnessing your powers and draining you dry. Your powers will then travel through the rods and into the orb before me, making it radioactive much like the ones you all came in contact with. Once the orb is fully charged, I will place my hands upon it and all of your powers will enter my body."

"But what if your body can't take the stress? That's a lot of power," I pointed out. "Maybe you will die too."

"If I do, then it will not have been in vain. It will have been in the name of science." He held up his hand triumphantly. "But I am quite confident I won't die, silly child," he said, looking down on me as though I wasn't very smart. "I will be the most powerful person in the universe."

His eyes looked beyond crazy now. He truly believed every word he said. He spread his arms wide and held his hands in the air. "I will be invincible!"

"But how are you going to contain our powers to harness them in the first place?" Kyle asked, finally able to speak.

"Look up. See that glass dome above you? Once I lower that and flip the switch on the orb, the process will begin. And nothing on this earth can penetrate that glass."

We needed to get our powers back before he lowered that dome. We needed to stop his insane evil plan. We needed a miracle!

# 15

## LET THE GAMES BEGIN!

Doctor Van Alstyne was getting ready to test the switch that fired up the orb before lowering the glass dome, when the room plunged into darkness. We heard shuffling about the room, and then a flashlight beam flicked on.

"Seems the FBI cut the power. Do they really think that will stop me? Then again, they still think Lance is the mastermind, so their amateur tactics really don't surprise me," he muttered to himself as he turned on a large battery-operated light in the center of the room. "Those bombs don't need power, and I have a generator they can't touch. Naïve fools." He left the room, probably to fire up the generator.

"Okay, guys, we have to act fast. We can't do anything as normal humans. Once he lowers that glass dome, we're doomed," I said. "We need to take out that box in the corner ceiling."

"But how without our powers?" Brent asked. "We don't have anything."

"We have Amy," I replied.

"Me?" Amy frowned. "What can I do?"

"You can pitch, can't you?" I asked.

She grinned widely. "Pitched a no-hitter in softball last spring. And that was *before* I became Athletica."

"That's what I figured." I grinned back. "Now we just need something heavy enough."

We all started looking around the room.

"What are we going to use?" Kyle asked. "Most everything's out of reach of our chain leashes."

"What about that huge watch you're wearing?" Francesca asked.

"No way. This is a Breitling, and my dad would kill me. You're the fashion-accessory expert," Kyle pointed out. "Use *your* watch."

"Not heavy enough," Francesca countered. "And you're not the only one who would be dead meat. My mom would flip if I ruined the birthday present she just gave me."

"What about artsy boy's shoes?" Gi asked. "Those suckers are humongo."

"Dude, are those lifts?" Warren gaped at Parker's feet.

"No! They have thick soles. My back kills me when I stand for hours painting, okay?" Parker's face flushed red, no roses in sight, as he glanced at Hope who stood beside him at about the same height. Without his "thick soles," she was probably a good inch taller than him.

"My back hurts me too," said Hope softly. "I slouch sometimes since I used to be on the tall side, but everyone has passed me now so I really don't need to anymore. It's a habit, I guess. Now I just look stupid."

"You don't look stupid to me," Parker said just as softly. "You look perfect."

"Cute, lover boy, but we don't have all day," Michaela

chimed in. "Hand them over so Amy can nail that box before Doctor Psycho gets back."

Parker quickly slipped a shoe off and handed it to Amy. Amy aimed, wound up, and then released. The heavy shoe went sailing through the air and hit the box dead center. It cracked but didn't break.

"You can do this, Amy," I said. "Parker, give her your other shoe."

He slipped his other shoe off and tossed it to Amy. She took a deep breath and went through the same motions, throwing the shoe even harder this time. The box split in half with a big spark and then hung uselessly in the air.

"*Yes!*" Brent yelled. "Good job, Amy."

The lights in the room flickered back to life, and we all looked at each other. The generator was on which meant Dr. Psycho would be back any second. I fired up my cell hand, called Gram, and quickly filled her in about Simon's uncle being a madman and holding us hostage. The door to the lab swung open, and the crazy doctor marched back inside.

I disconnected just as he resumed his place by the orb, not seeming to notice the dangling box in the corner. Or the fact that we all had our powers once more. Without a word, he hit a button on his control and the glass dome lowered over us, locking in place.

He was just getting ready to throw the switch that would fire up the orb and drain all our powers into the conductors in front of each of us, when his cell phone rang. He frowned, looking as though he were figuring out his next move, while he answered the phone.

"Special Agent Crawford, so glad to hear from you. I managed to escape Lance long enough to take your call, but he'll realize I'm gone shortly. I must get--" He paused and his face hardened, and then he shot me an accusing look.

His plans of coming off looking like a hero--the only lucky victim to survive--were over. Even if he did pull this off, he would be on the run for the rest of his life, and he knew it.

"You'll never catch me," he went on. "And I wouldn't try anything stupid, if I were you. I have nothing to lose. One wrong move, and I'll blow up the school, myself included. I've lost everything anyway, and if I can't have this, my life is over. Let me finish my work and walk away, and I just might let the children go after I finish with them."

He studied us all for a second and then said into the phone, "Give me a minute to step away from prying ears, and I'll give you a list of my demands." He walked out of the room and closed the door behind him.

"Sam, we have to do something. We can't let him win," Brent said.

"I know," I said on a shaky breath. "We can't give up, we just need a plan. We need to figure out a way to stop the conductors."

"I'm scared," said Hope.

"We're all scared," I said, and no one, not even Kyle, contradicted me, "but to pull this off, we have to be fearless. We might not be able to beat him on our own, but as a team, we can do anything. We just have to work together."

"Together." Francesca held her fist in the air.

One by one everyone else did the same.

"Okay, think," I said. "We all have our powers back, so we need to use what we've got."

"The glass is too thick for me to break on my own," Michaela said. "It's locked down tight. It won't open until the process is complete."

"So we let the doctor throw the switch and start the process," Brent said.

"Are you crazy, dude?" Warren gaped at him.

"Just hear me out," Brent added. "We just need the power of the conductors to build to the highest level. If they are blocked by something that won't conduct, then our powers won't be drained or travel to the orb. The pressure will cause the glass dome to explode. Right Sam? Pressure cookers have been known to do that?"

"Um, yeah, you could say that," I agreed, remembering all the times my internal pressure cooker had gotten too high because of Trevor and all the 911 calls I'd blocked. Pretty powerful stuff.

"What if *we* explode with it?" Kyle looked skeptical.

I used my computer brain and ran the scenario in my head. "We won't. We might get hurt a little, but we won't explode."

"I say we go for it," Gi said. "It's not like we have much of a choice."

"What do we have that's rubber? I only have metal on me," Ricky said.

"My stuff's hard plastic," Gi added.

"Will lacrosse balls work?" Amy asked.

"Perfect," I said. "Now we just have to stuff them in all the conductors so the holes are blocked. And hurry. We don't have much time."

"But how? None of us can reach," Francesca pointed out.

"Michaela can cut each of us loose from our chains while Amy collects enough lacrosse balls out of her Jell-O stomach. Parker can mark an x on each target. Gi can spray each opening with tacky paint. Warren can skate around, stuffing the balls inside the holes. Hope can clean up our mess so the doctor doesn't suspect what we're up to. And Kyle can rewind us if we make a mistake."

"What about me?" Ricky asked.

"You're going to wait until the conductor's have reached their maximum power level, and then you're going to play the loudest, highest opera-worthy note you can manage to help the glass explode."

I turned to Brent. "I need you to be ready. After we're free, I'm going to capture the doctor while you win us something to contain him. Everyone know what they are supposed to do?"

Everyone nodded, looking scared to death but ready. The time was now or never. Our lives depended on it.

"On three," I said, and the Phenoteens got to work.

By the time Dr. Psycho came back into the Lab, we were all standing just as he'd left us. Breathing slightly harder and sweating a bit more, but looking pretty much the same as we held our broken chains together so he wouldn't be able to tell.

"You'll never get away with this," I said, trying to distract him from inspecting us closer and figuring out what we were up to.

He narrowed his eyes at us and stared for what felt like forever, then finally walked over to the orb. "This is it. The moment I've waited a lifetime for. You should feel proud." He rubbed his hands together in anticipation and licked his lips, his eyes going wide and glazed. "You're about to be a part of history." He flipped the switch next to the orb, making it glow the same bright blue-green as the radioactive meteorite had back in Blue Lake.

Wind, energy and light began swirling around us inside the glass dome like an out-of-control strobe light. Our hair whipped around, stinging our faces and eyes, and the noise howled loudly. We all dropped our chains and covered our ears, yelling, the pain and pressure almost too much to bear.

The conductors before each of us started to shake, and the glass walls vibrated.

The mad-scientist doctor hadn't even noticed our broken chains or shaking conductors as he stood mesmerized, in a trancelike state. He held his hands out before him, hovering over the orb as it began to glow brighter. "Almost there, my precious, just a few ... more ... minutes."

"Now Ricky!" I shouted above the noise.

Ricky pulled his hands away from his ears, wincing against the pain but managing to transform his arms into an electric guitar with a powerful built-in amp. Ricky blasted a note so loud it had to have sent dogs howling and scurrying for cover up to thousands of miles away.

The glass dome shattered into a million pieces and we all dropped to the platform floor, covering our heads on terrified screams.

"*No!*" the doctor wailed, looking up in shock and confusion.

Glass was everywhere. The broken conductors continued to spark, pop, and hiss as they stood at crooked angles around the platform.

"What have you done?" the doctor stared in horror at his life's work, destroyed beyond repair. His eyes changed from shock to horror to grief to...to rage!

# 16

## AND THE WINNER IS

"It's all your fault, Digital Diva," Dr. Van Alstyne said. "And now you're going to pay." He held up his gun and pointed it in my direction.

We might be superheroes, and our suits might be bullet-proof, but our suits didn't cover every inch of our skin.

He fired off a round, and my GPS brain kicked into gear, the mental parts grinding and shifting as it calculated exactly where the bullet was going to hit me. I downloaded a demonstration of how to move like the people in *The Matrix* movie. My body arched backwards, and I nearly did a backbend as the bullet missed me by a mere inch. My bones remained soft in a rubber-band-like state. I could only hope this side-effect wouldn't last long and that my bones would harden again quickly.

"Impressive, but are your friends as impressive as you?" The doctor turned his gun on the rest of the Phenoteens.

He tried to hit Warren, but Warren popped out his Motocross wheels and gunned his dirt bike, burning rubber. He peeled out across the floor, hit a ramp, and sailed over the doctor's head, landing on the other side of the room.

The doctor nicked Warren's back tire, and Warren let out a yelp. His wheel transformed back to a foot and Warren limped on his bleeding heel and took cover behind a counter.

"You've been hit!" Michaela gasped.

"Ah, it's just a scratch." Warren smiled. "I knew you cared."

She rolled her eyes, then hurried over to fix his flat-tire foot. "I care about getting out of here alive."

The doctor headed in their direction to finish what he'd started, but Ricky threw a drumstick at him, hitting him in the head. That just made Dr. Psycho angrier.

"You stupid boy. You think you can beat me?"

Gi jumped in front of Ricky and fired off a round of air soft BB pellets.

The doctor just smiled evilly. "My vest is bulletproof. Is yours?"

Gi looked down at her paintball vest and her eyes widened. She grabbed Ricky's hand and ran behind a long row of metal cabinets as the madman shot two more bullets.

"You can run but you can't hide," he said in a scary voice like something had possessed him.

"I don't hide from anyone," Francesca said, stepping back onto the platform. "I'm used to being center stage, doc." She shot out a stream of scalding water in his direction, but he stepped aside at the last second. "I always loved a good encore." She turned the other way, ready to blast him with her blow-dryer ear.

The doctor raised his gun in her direction. "It's time for your curtain call. You're not good enough for an encore, my dear." He shot off a round, but Brent tackled her at the last second, rolling her off the platform.

The shot ricocheted and hit an experiment in a Bunsen

burner, causing a minor explosion and igniting the liquid in the burner. "Look what you did, you crazy man," Hope said, racing over. She put out the fire, cleaning up the mess in the process.

When the doctor tried to shoot Hope, Parker blasted his internal light into the doctor's eyes and the bullet missed its target. The battle continued, and I realized the focus was off me. There had to be something I could do. I looked around the room and saw a stack of textbooks. There had to be something useful in there.

I stretched and bounced my way over there, my bones finally hardening enough for me to flip through the books. Fluttering my eyelashes, I activated my speed reader, horrified when they grew another millimeter. My eyes finally landed on a page with a Nobel Prize winner.

*That's it!* I thought.

I downloaded a formula at lightning speed, information entering my cerebrum. Whizzing into my lobes for processing, it then shot into my gray matter for storage, increasing my intelligence way beyond genius mode. A nasty sulfur taste lingered on my tongue and sulfur smell hovered in my nose, but at least I now knew exactly what to do. I just had to find the ingredients.

With no time to search through all the cupboards, I fired up my x-ray vision by blinking my eyes. Staring at the closed white cup boards, I concentrated hard. Light shot into my eyes, forming an upside-down image on my retinas, and then my retinas transformed the light into nerve signals. My Electro Wave brain turned the images right side up and told me exactly what was inside each cupboard.

There was just enough to make one dose.

Now that my bones were completely back to normal, I

gathered the ingredients, mixed the concoction rapidly, and loaded it into a spray canister.

"This is ridiculous," Amy snapped. "Pause, Kyle."

Kyle hit pause on the professor, and Amy nailed him with a dodgeball. Then everyone scrambled to the other side of the room. Everyone except me. The pause function went off seconds later, and the doctor doubled over in agony. Quickly recovering, he stood up and locked eyes on me. As he lifted his gun in my direction, I slipped a gas mask on and sprayed the canister in his face.

"What in the world?" He coughed and wheezed.

Brent beat a video game and a massive cage appeared out of nowhere, slamming down around the doctor.

The doctor managed to turn to us with sheer evilness in his bleary eyes. He held up the gun and pulled the trigger.

Click.

Gi just laughed. "Six bullets. You're out, game over."

Dr. Van Alstyne kept pulling the trigger, but all he got was an empty clicking sound echoed throughout the lab over and over again like a skip in a record. He looked stunned that he had been beaten. "Game not over," he said and pulled out the detonator to the bomb.

Our eyes widened as he pressed the button just seconds before collapsing to the floor.

"Oh, my God, you killed him," Francesca said.

"Not dead, just sleeping," I clarified as I pulled off the gas mask. "But we'll be dead if we don't find a way out of here before that bomb goes off."

WE ALL RAN AROUND THE ROOM TESTING THE DOORS AND windows and locks, but it was no use. I called Gram, and she put Dark Shades man on the phone.

"Maxwell here."

"This is Sam. The crazy doctor detonated the bomb."

"Unlock the doors, and we'll send in the bomb squad."

"I can't. The building is still on lockdown, and we can't get out."

"Do you know where he hid the bombs?"

"No."

"Is there any way you can get him to tell you the codes to unlock the building?"

I glanced at the sleeping doctor. "Um, not before twenty minutes, and by then it will probably be too late." My stomach churned as I realized we might not make it out alive.

"Why twenty minutes?" Maxwell asked.

"Sleeping gas." My brilliant idea didn't seem so brilliant any more.

"Clever. Okay, then. Listen to me closely, Samantha. You all have special powers. There has to be a way for you to get out. You're Phenoteens, remember? Use your resources." He paused. "You can do this. You just have to stay calm and use your brains."

Fearless, I thought. *I can do this.* "Okay, but you might want to stand back just in case." I disconnected.

"Well?" Francesca asked, looking at me with wide eyes.

In fact, they all were staring at me with hope, expecting me to know the answers. I couldn't let them down.

"Well, there's no way we can reverse what happened because it's been too long. And the walls are too thick to cut through. Our only hope is Brent."

"Me?"

"Yeah. Think you can win us something big enough to blast our way through the doors?"

He thought about it, and then his face lit up. "I've got just the thing. Hang on." He fused his hands together and played an army video game faster than I'd ever seen him play. Suddenly a massive tank slammed on the ground in front of us. "Will that do?"

"That's perfect," I said.

"Only, who knows how to drive that thing?" Kyle raised his eyebrows doubtfully.

"Me," I said, and they all looked impressed. "Let's just say I've had some experience in the driving department." I laughed. "Now quit gawking at me and hop in." I climbed to the top and opened the latch.

Everyone scrambled inside except Michaela. "What about him?" she asked, jerking her head in Dr. Van Alstyne's direction. "I know he deserves it, but are we just gonna leave him here?"

"No," I said, "because that would make us just like him." We heard the first explosion off in the distance, and I sucked in a breath. "Come on, hurry." I jumped down, and she followed me.

We grabbed the chains the doctor had used to bind us and fastened them around the cage he was inside of. Then we hooked them to the back of our tank. Michaela transformed her hand into a welder and welded the chains together. "There, that should hold."

"Perfect. Now quick, get inside." I held the door and then climbed in after her, lowering the top.

Once we had the top secured, I took the driver's seat. Downloading instructions on how to drive an army tank created a camouflage rash that covered my hands, but I'd worry about it later. I fired up the tank as the explosions sounded closer.

With me gunning the engine and maneuvering the hand controls, the tank rolled forward. I picked up speed, dragging the cage behind us, and crashed through the lab doors. We barreled down the hallway as fast as the tank would roll, the explosions getting closer and closer.

"Hurry, Sam, I can feel the heat in here," Brent said from the seat beside me.

"Good, I hope it singes the doctor's eyebrows off for putting us in this situation," Francesca said.

"I'm trying to hurry, but this thing only has one speed," I stated.

We came to the end of a hallway that went both left and right. "Which way?" Gi asked.

"Left," Ricky said.

"No right," Kyle said.

"Neither one of you knows what you're talking about." Amy huffed. "Sam?"

I brought up the floor plans for the school, but this section wasn't clear. "I'm not sure. There might have been renovations made."

"What are we going to do?" Hope asked.

Parker hugged her. "We're going to die."

"Not on my watch," I said. "Brace yourselves!"

Everyone grabbed onto anything they could, and I closed my eyes as we crashed through the side of the building. Brick and mortar flew everywhere, but the tank made it through. We had driven about a hundred yards away from the building when the last and biggest bomb exploded.

"You did it," someone said in awe.

"No, *we* did it," I said, turning to look at my fellow Phenoteens. "We're free."

The crowd cheered, and our parents rushed toward us.

My jaw fell open in stunned surprise. How had our parents gotten here so fast? I googled the Internet in my brain for news reports of the incident. The FBI had used military planes and helicopters that travel at insane speeds to fly our parents in immediately, fearing the worst but hoping for the best.

Dark Shades Man.

A new soft spot settled in my heart for the man I once despised. Maybe he wasn't so horrible after all. We opened the hatch and climbed out, rushing to our parents and hugging them tight. Answering any questions would come later. Right now we were just glad to be alive, and everyone seemed to sense that.

I suddenly remembered I had unfinished business. I walked around to the back of the tank and stared at a now slightly singed but fully alert Doctor Psycho.

"This isn't over, Digital Diva." He stared at me long and hard until the hairs on the back of my neck stood at attention. "We *will* meet again someday."

"Doubt it," I said.

"Haven't you learned by now that nothing's impossible?"

I didn't want to believe him, but something in my gut told me he was right.

# 17

# STRINGS

The police had taken Simon's crazy uncle away in handcuffs. The rest of us were surrounded by our families, watching the fire department put out the flames of IPR. It would be a long time before the school was fully rebuilt.

Our parents had been outside the whole time, anxiously awaiting the outcome. And miraculously, the program's real purpose remained a secret. Everyone wondered a little about the Army tank and the cage, but they still thought IPR was just a school for gifted students who had skills like perfect IQ's and photographic memories. If they only knew--we were phenomenons, all right.

Phenomenal Superheroes, that is!

"Oh Sam, I'm so sorry," Mom said, hugging me tight once more. "I never should have insisted you go to this school. I was only trying to help you."

"I know, Mom, and it's okay. You didn't know what would happen. None of us did." I smiled at her reassuringly. "If I hadn't come to this school, I would never have made such special friends." I shot Gram a look, and she winked at me. A special bond had formed among us all, and we had agreed we would remain the Phenoteens until we found a safe way to reverse this whole mess we were in.

"You're mother's right, Sam." Dad hugged me again as well. "You could have been killed, and it's all our fault."

"It's not your fault." I looked up at him. "It's Simon's uncle's fault. He's insane."

"You're not kidding. He kept spouting off about super-heroes and a government conspiracy to steel his life's work." Dad sighed. "I just feel bad for Simon. He worshiped that man."

"Me, too." Simon would need Maria now more than ever. "What about the real fusion expert, Dr. Guggenheim?" I asked. "Any news on him?"

"He's safe and sound. They found him in a small cabin that belonged to Simon's uncle's assistant. I guess she's been in love with dr. Van Alstyne for years and would have done just about anything he asked. She's been arrested as well, and the real Dr. Guggenheim is back home, safe and sound with his family." Dad's eyes misted. "Like you will be soon. And I'm moving to Blue Lake for good this time."

"You mean you and Mom--"

"No, I mean you and me. Baby steps, princess. Baby steps."

"Okay, Dad." At least it was a start, and I would take whatever I could get.

"I'm going to go take the few things you have left and put them on the plane along with ours. Your mom just went to finish signing you out. And I think your grandmother went to have a word with Agent Maxwell." Dad chuckled. "Lord only knows what for."

I had a pretty good idea she was telling him off. I grinned, and once we were alone, Mel stepped up and hugged me the tightest of all. "I'm so glad you're coming home."

"Me too." I hugged her back, not shocked in the least that she was there. I'd seen it all when I'd hacked into the FBI site and watched the video. Leave it to Mel to find a way to sneak on board. By the time the FBI had caught her, it had been too late. She really was the best sidekick ever.

I pulled away from her and said, "Since the government couldn't even keep us safe, they agreed to cancel the program and let us go home. Plus it will take a long time to fix the academy."

"Just like that? You're free to go home with no strings or anything?" She looked surprised.

"I know. It seems too easy, but that's what they said." I shrugged. "Come on, I want to introduce you to my new friends." I grabbed her hand, pulled her over to a group of people, and then introduced her to the gang.

One by one as they left, she asked for more details and I filled her in on who they "really" were.

"There has to be a story there. I've never seen two people bicker more," Mel said.

"Kyle aka King Cable is too gorgeous for words, but he can be a major control freak with his hand remote. He's getting better. The toned girl beside him is Amy aka Athletica. He loves to torment her, but she can hold her own. There's a reason she always gets chosen most valuable player."

"Awww, who are they? They look so sweet together." Mel pointed to the couple walking out hand in hand.

"Parker aka Picasso Kid has it bad for Hope aka Home

Ec Helper. He sprouts heart-and-flower tattoos every time he's around her, but he can't kiss her because of the toxic cleaning solution in her mouth. It's too bad really. They make such a cute couple, and she likes him back."

"What about them? He seems like a devil, and she looks like she's ready to hammer him."

"You've got that right. Warren aka Wheels is cool, but he loves to mess around. Michaela aka Mechanica is the serious hard-working sort, and gets frustrated with his antics easily, which makes him want to do them all the more."

"And those two? They look like they could butt heads a lot."

"Gi aka Gunner Girl is a tough nut who shoots first and talks later. She lives to bust Ricky aka Rock Star's strings, while he loves to pull her trigger. But don't you worry, she knows just how to send his instrument out of tune when he steps too far out of line." I laughed.

"Wow, who's she?" Mel asked. "She's beautiful."

"That is my roommate, Francesca aka Fashionista. She reminds me of you, only she can be seriously high maintenance. She liked Brent aka X-Boy, but he only liked her as a friend. Speaking of which, I didn't get to tell you yet."

"What?"

"He kissed me."

"Get out!"

"For real," I said. "He goes from Mr. Ordinary to Mr. Adorable with just a smile. You'll see what I mean when you meet him."

"So how was it?"

"Well, I thought he could make me forget about Trevor, but it was the weirdest thing. We both agreed it was like kissing a brother or sister, so we decided to be just friends. I can't wait for you to meet him."

"Speaking of just friends, Trevor and Scott broke off their dates with the Petterelli twins. Trevor was just trying to forget about you, too, since you left without saying good-bye, but everyone knows he really likes you still."

"What about Scott? Does that mean you two are back together?"

She frowned. "No way. I'm still so mad at him. Trevor had a reason to ask that girl to the dance, Scott didn't. He just follows in Trevor's footsteps, trying to be just like him."

"So, what about the dance then? Aren't you still going?"

"Nope. What about you? You'll be home in time now. Why don't you ask Trevor?"

"You know why." My eyes met hers, and a feeling of helplessness hit me hard. "I still can't date him. He would try to kiss me, and I would set off alarms and block 911 calls and be sent to the rescue. Digital Diva needs a break."

"Bummer. This is the biggest dance of the year, and now neither of us is going."

Brent stepped away from his parents, spotted us, and then said, "Be right back," to them, and jogged over to join us.

"Hi, I'm Brent." He smiled widely, blasting Mel with a Mr. Adorable smile. "And you have *got* to be Mel. I've heard a lot about you, sidekick." He grinned.

Mel just stood there, looking dumbfounded. I nudged her in the shoulder with a giggle, and she snapped to attention. "Cawesome ... I mean cool ... or awesome ... or whatever." She snorted and then slapped a hand over her mouth.

Brent arched a brow at me.

I grinned. "Didn't you know? Cawesome is all the rage where we come from, too."

He laughed. "Sounds like a cool place. Speaking of Blue Lake, I just found out we're going on vacation. My parents think I need a break. Guess where I asked them to take me?" Brent's eyes sparkled with mischief.

"I can't imagine," I said.

"Some ski resort in the Adirondacks called Blue Peak."

"No way," Mel finally spoke. "Blue Lake is really close to Blue Peak. Maybe Sam and I could show you around."

His gaze settled on Mel and lingered with interest. "Sure, we could double date or something." He looked at me. "What about that Trevor guy you told me about?"

"That's a great idea, Sam." Mel leaned forward and whispered, "He's not seeing anyone anymore, and I could use a sidekick right about now."

"I can't date. Remember?" I hissed back at her, but Brent overheard.

"Haven't you learned anything from hanging out with me, Fabulastic Sam?" He shot me a meaningful look. "Where there's a will, there's always a way." His gaze landed on Mel, and he smiled slowly. "Ever heard of EMP?"

"No," Mel said, sounding fascinated and staring up at Brent in wonder. "What is it?"

"You'll see."

———

BRENT TALKED HIS PARENTS INTO TAKING THEIR ADIRONDACK ski vacation two weeks later so it would fall on Blue Lake Junior High School's winter dance. He had asked Mel to go as his date, much to Scott's dismay and Mel's delight. She looked stunning with her auburn curls in an updo and her emerald-green silk dress falling just below her knees. Her smile was beaming as he twirled her around the floor.

Meanwhile Scott sat in the corner glaring at Trevor, with pouting Petterelli twins on either side of him. Served him right after what he had done to Mel. She would forgive him in time, but for now, she was enjoying a little payback. Besides, she really liked Brent, and he seemed to like her.

I couldn't help be a little jealous. Mel and Brent could date freely because she knew about his powers, where I could only date Trevor if Brent was in town. And since I couldn't explain why, Trevor really didn't get it. I knew one day he would get tired of my hot and cold behavior toward him and give up on me for good. But until that day came, I planned to enjoy every minute I got to spend with him.

I rested my cheek on his shoulder while he held me close and we danced. It was the last song of the night, and the dance was almost over. I'd had the best time. My heart sank. Trevor was never going to understand why I would refuse to go out with him again after we'd had such an amazing night. I sighed.

"I'm glad you're back, Sam," his voice rumbled from within his chest.

I looked up into his amazing blue eyes, and the butter-flies danced in my stomach just like they always did when he was near me. "Me too," I said softly and meant it.

He looked so good with his wavy brown hair brushing his shoulders and his sparkling blue eyes staring down at me. His dark blue suit looked great beside my lavender dress. I felt like a princess and had Brent to thank for giving me this one night. But all too soon I knew my fairy tale would be over.

Trevor's smile slipped. "You look sad. How come?"

"No reason. I just don't want this night to end, I guess." If only I had something to remember it by. I gazed up at him, hoping he'd get the hint. The last time he'd kissed me, I had been half unconscious. But with Brent here, I could be fully awake and experience the full effect.

There was nothing I wanted more.

"It's not over yet," Trevor said, his head slowly lowering toward mine as though reading my thoughts.

"Wait." I laughed nervously, and he looked at me warily.

"You're not going to run again, are you?"

"No, and I mean it this time. Just...don't move. I'll be right back." I ran over to Brent, tapped him on the shoulder, and didn't have to say a word.

He grabbed Mel's hand, and said, "Come on, sidekick, we've got work to do." His eyes met mine. "Wait until the lights flicker. That will be your signal." Then they took off to the coat room.

I ran back to Trevor who looked at me a little strangely and I said, "Where were we?"

"Uh, nowhere." He shoved his hands in his pockets.

"Really, are you sure?" I kept glancing up at the lights.

His eyes followed mine and his eyebrow arched. "Yeah, I'm sure. I can't remember, and besides, the moment's probably all wrong now."

Just then the lights flickered.

I bit my bottom lip, making a decision. "I think the moment's perfect," I said and reached up, putting my arms around his neck and planting my lips on his.

He just sat there in stunned surprise and then snapped out of it and kissed me back for real this time. Fireworks went off behind my eyelids, my heart pounded, and my toes tingled--but my feet stayed firmly planted on the floor. Nothing brotherly or sisterly about that kiss. The EMP had worked, and I owed Brent big-time.

It felt great to be free.

Trevor and I broke apart and smiled shyly at each other,

and then my cell hand vibrated. I jumped, almost forgetting for a moment that I was anything except a normal girl.

"What's wrong?" he asked.

"Nothing. Everything's perfect. I've just got to check in with my mom. You know how she gets."

"Boy, do I ever." He looked a little wary. "I've seen her in action when she was dating my dad. Don't get me wrong, she's nice enough and all, but she's your mom. If they ever hooked up for good, we'd be like step-brother and sister. All I can say is thank God that's over."

"Weird," I said, shuddering, and so thankful my mom was single again. Because that meant there was still hope for her and Dad.

"Yeah," Trevor confirmed.

We both laughed off the awkward moment, and Brent and Mel joined us. "We'll be right back," I said, grabbing Mel's hand and pulling her toward the girl's bathroom.

"We'll be here waiting," Trevor said. "For however long it takes."

There was a world of meaning packed into that one sentence. I just smiled as we walked off, knowing I had no answer for when that might be.

"What's going on?" Mel asked.

"I'm not sure," I answered. "I just got a text." Once we were in the bathroom, I checked under the stalls and made sure we were alone. Pulling off my glove, I gasped. It's from the government.

"What's it say?"

I read the text:

YOUR MENTOR IS ON HIS WAY, AND HE WILL DELIVER A SPECIAL *beeper. The IPR program might have been cancelled, but*

*Project Phenoteen is still very much alive. You will be hearing from us soon.*


"BUT I THOUGHT YOU WERE FREE?" MEL ASKED, LOOKING confused and a little worried.

"Me too," I answered in dread and then added, "but I guess not. Freedom isn't really free if there are strings."

# ABOUT THE AUTHOR

Kari Lee Townsend is a National Bestselling Author of mysteries & a tween superhero series. She also writes romance and women's fiction as Kari Lee Harmon. With a background in English education, she's now a full-time writer, wife to her own superhero, mom of 3 sons, 1 darling diva, 1 daughter-in-law & 2 lovable fur babies. These days you'll find her walking her dogs or hard at work on her next story, living a blessed life.

## ALSO BY THE AUTHOR

Sleeping in the Middle

MERRY SCROOGE-MAS SERIES

Naughty or Nice

Sleigh Bells Ring

Jingle All The Way

LAKE HOUSE TREASURES SERIES

The Beginning

Amber

Meghan

Brook